Goddess

EOS
THE
LIGHTHEARTED

Goddess Girls

EOS
THE
LIGHTHEARTED

JOAN HOLUB & SUZANNE WILLIAMS

Aladdin

NEW YORK   LONDON   TORONTO   SYDNEY   NEW DELHI

ALADDIN

An imprint of Simon & Schuster Children's Publishing Division

1230 Avenue of the Americas, New York, New York 10020

First Aladdin paperback edition December 2018

Text copyright © 2018 Joan Holub and Suzanne Williams

Cover illustration copyright © 2018 by Glen Hanson

Also available in an Aladdin hardcover edition.

For information about special discounts for bulk purchases, please contact Simon & Schuster Special Sales at 1-866-506-1949 or business@simonandschuster.com.

The Simon & Schuster Speakers Bureau can bring authors to your live event. For more information or to book an event contact the Simon & Schuster Speakers Bureau at 1-866-248-3049 or visit our website at www.simonspeakers.com.

Book designed by Karin Paprocki

The text of this book was set in Baskerville.

Manufactured in the United States of America 1118 OFF

2 4 6 8 10 9 7 5 3 1

Library of Congress Control Number 2018947644

ISBN 978-1-4814-7021-6 (hc)

ISBN 978-1-4814-7020-9 (pbk)

ISBN 978-1-4814-7022-3 (eBook)

Goddess Girls readers are pink*!*

To Emily and Grondine Family, Koko Y., Keny Y., Amelia G.,
Cathlyn K., Zellah C., Camren N., Stephanie T., Christine D-H.,
Khanya S., Olive Jean D., Lillia L., Ellis T., Holly N.,
Virginia J, Shelby J., Samantha J., Andrade Family, Jenny C.,
Kira L., Sloane G., Leah G., Denise L., Yomara L., Emily G.,
Abby C., Jocey B., Jasmine G., Xiomara M., Akira W.,
Ilicia M., Gelila Z., Ruby G., Samantha C., McKenna W.,
Aurora-Joyce P., Elia P., Evilynn R., Brenda T., Joselin H.,
Leilah G., Genesis M., Madeline W., Elizabeth K.,
Julianna H'O., Julez O., Samantha S., Mackenzie S., Ivan S.,
Caitlin R., Hannah R., Elna B., Kristen S., Samantha K.,
Allie K., Danielle H., Lana W., Katlyn G., Rachel L., Sarah M.,
Aurora S., Sassy S., Elle S., Josi S., Lorelai M., Kira L.,
Shelby Lynn J., Samantha Grace J., Virginia Anna J., and you!

—J. H. and S. W.

CONTENTS

Goddess Girls

EOS
THE
LIGHTHEARTED

1

The Dawn

Eos, THE GODDESS OF THE DAWN, FLUTTERED into the sky on feathery white wings. Her bright, saffron-colored robe, its hem embroidered with lovely blue flowers, ruffled in the breeze as she moved up and up, preparing to bring forth the morning. A lighthearted inner joy filled her, as it always did at this moment. In mere seconds she would share some of that joy with the world around her.

High above her, Nyx, the goddess of the night, stood in her horse-drawn chariot reeling in her magical cape. Both girls were twelve years old, but though the same age, they were pretty much opposites. Dawn and darkness. Yet they'd become good friends.

Nyx's dark cape and the plum-colored gown she wore were studded with stars that twinkled and flashed as she expertly tugged her cape down from the heavens. Her clever hands worked fast, folding the rapidly shrinking cape to make it smaller and smaller. Once it was the size of a sandwich, she would pocket it. Her nightly job completed, she would then go home to sleep in the Underworld.

Eos felt her heart clench at the mere thought of that deep and gloomy place underground. And a familiar "sad-mad" feeling that had nothing to do with Nyx welled up inside her. As always, Eos quickly squashed that feeling before it could swallow her happiness.

Then, aware that Nyx's cape was nearly folded now, she brought her attention back to the task at hand. It was almost time for her to take over from her friend to bring forth the dawn!

Nyx looked down, and the girls' eyes caught. Eos grinned and wiggled her rosy fingers in a wave that caused long, squiggly lines of pink vapor to drift outward from her fingertips.

"Was it a good night?" Eos called up.

"Yes, thanks!" Nyx called back. "Also, I have big news! There's finally going to be . . ." Her attention wandered from her folding, and she made a wrinkle. She paused to smooth it, then went on breathlessly, "Sorry. I'd better keep my mind on what I'm doing.

I'll toss down the notescroll I wrote you when I finish with my cape. It'll explain."

"Pink!" Eos called back, which was her word for "cool." "Can't wait to read it!" *What could the news be?* she wondered. Since the two girls worked opposite schedules, their interactions were brief, and they never had much time to actually chat. It would be weird for the world if darkness and dawn lingered together too long. So mostly they communicated through the notescrolls they tossed each other as Nyx was leaving for bed and Eos was beginning her day.

Speaking of beginning her day, she really needed to get a move on! Graceful as a dancer, Eos raised both arms over her head. With gentle flicks of her wrists she sent glistening rays of pink, purple, and orange to fan out along the horizon. While she worked, she swayed from side to side, sometimes twirling with happiness as she sent out her colors to paint the sky with the misty, drifting hues of dawn.

Though she performed this same action every day, she never grew tired of it. In fact, the satisfaction she got from watching her colors spread was her greatest joy in life. (This was a feeling Nyx understood, since she did something sort of similar with the aid of her cape.)

Eos loved to imagine her colorful dawn filling all beings who were awake to see it with energy and hope for the new day ahead. Not that everyone was an early riser like her, of course. But in her opinion, late risers were really missing out!

Nyx had finished folding her cape, and now she slipped it into the pocket of her gown. "Time to head for home, Erebus," she called to her swift and loyal horse. He gave a whinny and then took off, mane flying. As Erebus swooped past Eos, Nyx reached over the side of her purple-and-gold chariot and tossed the notescroll.

"Have a good day!" she called to Eos. "Hope you can come!"

"Hope you can come"? What was that all about? Eos wondered. Too busy with her work to catch the scroll just then, she watched it drop to the ground far beneath her. She took careful note of its approximate location, planning to retrieve it after her work was at an end.

About twenty minutes later, her older brother, Helios, appeared in the eastern sky. Crowned with the corona of the sun, he stood tall in his chariot, skillfully guiding his fiery horses. His purple robes billowed out behind him. It was his job to carry the sun across the sky each day. And his appearance meant that her brief duty was nearly done.

Eos gave one last happy twirl. Then, with ballerina-like movements, she gracefully lowered her arms. Slowly she crossed them over her chest, her fingers pulling in the last of her misty, colorful vapor. Her job complete, the dawn now faded to a faint pink glow that eased into the blue sky of morning.

From start to finish her dawn-making never took more than thirty minutes. That was only a fraction of the time that her brother's and Nyx's jobs took. Or her sister Selene's job, for Selene was goddess of the moon. Half an hour was perfect, really. Because if creating dawn had taken much longer, Eos would've had a hard time doing it. Not just because her arms would get tired. But mostly because her restless, curious mind liked to hop quickly from one thing to another.

She often wished she had better brain control. It was just that she was interested in *so* many things! Whenever something new caught her interest, she'd read up on it to learn as much as she could. Then, if the subject required practice, like knitting or playing the flute (two topics that had intrigued her in the past), she'd practice for hours each day. Eventually some other new subject would catch her attention, and she'd hop to the new one while abandoning the old.

Sometimes she wished she was more like Tithonus, a mortal boy who was her very best friend. He lived next door, and they went to Oceanus Middle School together. Now, *that* boy knew how to concentrate. And he had exactly one interest. Bugs!

As she watched the faint pink glow of her dawn dissolve completely, Eos suddenly remembered the scroll Nyx had dropped. Her eyes darted low to scour the ground for it. There it was!

She fluttered down and picked it up. Notescroll in hand, she flapped her feathery white wings and took to the air again. She had to be at school in thirty minutes! She'd have to read Nyx's notescroll later.

As she zoomed homeward to grab her school things, Eos recited to herself the names of various Greek cities, mountains, and rivers. She had a geography quiz second period. "Greece's four largest cities are Athens, Sparta, Thebes, and Corinth," she murmured. "The tallest mountain peak in Greece is Mount Olympus."

From this high in the air, that very mountain was easily visible now in the distance. The glint of Helios's sunlight lit the white polished stones of the five-story Mount Olympus Academy building that stood atop it. Many goddessgirls and godboys, as well as some mortals, attended that amazing school, but going there had never been one of Eos's dreams.

She had no desire to meet that dumb Zeus, who was the MOA principal. So what if he was King of the Gods and Ruler of the Heavens! He had earned the number one spot on her do-not-like list. Because he was totally responsible for that sad-mad thing she didn't like to think about! (It was actually a sad-mad-*dad* thing.) And she could never ever forgive Zeus for that. Not that he knew or cared.

Eos's neighborhood came into view below. She zoomed toward the blue-tiled roof of her bright yellow home and down into its enclosed humongous stone courtyard. Quickly, she landed in her mom's garden, which bordered the square mosaic-tiled courtyard on all four sides.

"Be careful not to trample my irises!" her mom, Theia, warned, pointing to some purple flowers near Eos. Trowel in hand, her mom had been kneeling in the dirt, rooting out weeds.

"Okay," Eos said, automatically folding in her white wings to tuck at her back. She tightened her hold on Nyx's notescroll as she hopped over the clump of purple flowers. At school she'd learned that the flowers were named after Iris, goddess of the rainbow and a student at Mount Olympus Academy.

She shot a glance at her mom, who'd gone back to her weeding. As usual, even when gardening, she looked dressed to attend a fancy party. She was wearing a glittery, sequined gold gown. A gold necklace embedded with precious gems including rubies, emeralds, and diamonds encircled her neck. The goddess of shiny things, she adored gowns that sparkled and all kinds of precious metals and jewels. She'd made that necklace herself.

Gardening and jewelry-making were Theia's two favorite hobbies, but she had many more. Just like Eos, her mom had lots of interests and was always doing something. They were both so busy it sometimes seemed like they didn't get to say more than a few words to each other all day.

Theia looked up as Eos hopped over a potted plant. "Good job this morning, by the way," she said, smiling. "Your dawn was gorgeous!"

"Thanks," said Eos.

"Your lunch is on the kitchen table," her mom went on. "I packed a daybreak-delight sandwich."

Eos ducked her head, and an awkward pause fell between them. "Daybreak-delight" had been her dad's nickname for the sandwiches he used to make her when she was little. They were peanut butter and jelly, with sliced banana in between. The sandwich had reminded them both of him, a topic Eos tried to avoid big-time. Her mom knew that.

She hadn't liked it when her mom kept trying to talk about him in those first years after he left them. Finally Eos had started covering her ears so she wouldn't hear and singing *lalalala*. After that, she'd made her mom promise not to bring him up anymore. Though disappointed, her mom had kept that promise. Just as Eos kept *her* promises. Just as her dad had *not*.

He'd broken his most important promise of all! His promise to come home after the war. A war that had put Zeus in power on Mount Olympus. But when the war ended, her dad did *not* come home.

Her gaze shot to a trophy that stood on a pedestal

in a corner of the garden. It was a prestigious award her dad had once won for his ability to cast spells. If he was so great at spell-casting, why hadn't he cast one to bring himself home? she'd wondered more than once.

"Great, thanks. Gotta hurry or I'll be late for school!" Eos said to Theia at last, breaking the awkward silence between them. Then she sped off abruptly before her mom got any ideas about bring-ing up the taboo dad subject.

Eos made a beeline for the large urn that stood at the very center of the tiled courtyard, feeling glad she always had so much to do. Staying busy kept her from dwelling on sad-mad-dad thoughts, though they still tended to pop up when she least expected them. It was almost like there was a jack-in-the-box of sad-mad feelings in the back of her mind, ready to spring forth at the slightest trigger.

She came to a stop before the three-foot tall terra-cotta urn. Decorated with a glazed black scene of women filling and carrying water jars at a fountain, it had a wide body that curved from its base up to its narrow, openmouthed top. And it was through this top that Eos intended to go, with the help of a little goddessgirl magic.

Twirling in slow circles that gradually spun faster and faster, she soon became a tornado of pink vapor. Quickly she whirled herself in through the opening at the top of the urn. Once she touched down inside it, she morphed from vapor into herself again, only a much smaller self now. Still feeling like she was spinning in circles, she stood for a few seconds till the dizziness passed.

She loved that this urn was all hers. It was her own special private place—her bedroom! Near the middle of the round room stood her comfy bed. It was piled with colorful pillows stuffed with soft feathers. A pink-painted wardrobe with a floral design sat on one side of the bed, a matching desk on the other. Built-in shelves filled with scrollbooks and knickknacks curved against the wall beyond the foot of the bed. Her favorite knickknack was a sparkly star-shaped ornament that Nyx had given her.

After grabbing the schoolwork and textscrolls she'd left on top of her desk, Eos stuffed them into her schoolbag, along with Nyx's notescroll. Though she and her belongings had shrunk to fit inside the urn, they would expand to normal size again once outside it.

"Guess that's everything," Eos murmured, taking one last look around her urn-room. Holding onto her schoolbag, she twirled in circles till she and her stuff became pink vapor. Then she swirled up and out through the neck of the urn, rising directly into the sky above the open courtyard.

Drat! She'd forgotten her lunch. She swooped low again. After zooming through the house to grab it, Eos yelled, "Bye, Mom!" Then she headed out into the lovely day she had created.

2
Tithonus

Eos raised her hand to knock on the red door of the small whitewashed stone house next to her own home. Before she could knock, however, the door was flung open. A boy wearing a light green tunic and leather sandals stood before her. Hanging from the leather cord that belted his tunic was a magnifying glass. As usual.

Grinning, Tithonus said, "Hey, Busy Bee!"

That was a nickname he sometimes called her.

She grinned back at him. "Happy dawn, Bug Boy. Sorry I'm late. Had to go back for my lunch."

He nodded and stepped out on the porch. "No prob. Let's get going, though." As they headed off for school, Tithonus began telling her about an unusual bug he'd come across yesterday. "It had two sets of transparent wings and a long iridescent green body. Some kind of dragonfly, but not one I've seen before. And it had . . ."

Eos smiled to herself as he went on describing the bug. Tithonus had been obsessed with bugs for as long as she could remember, even in preschool. His interest in them had rubbed off on her some, but she'd never be as passionate about creepy-crawly things as he was. Still, she admired his unwavering enthusiasm for bugs and his ability to observe them for long periods of time. Especially since doing anything for a long time was practically impossible for her with her busy mind always hopping around to something new.

Another thing she admired—*appreciated*, really—about Tithonus was that he was not in awe of her being a goddessgirl. She was the only one at their middle school! Unlike other students, who were all in awe of her, he would give her a hard time if she acted weird. Or tease her out of a bad mood, though never in a mean way. Maybe he dared such things because he wasn't just a mortal. He was a mortal prince! His family (and only he and his mom were left of it) no longer had a kingdom, however.

Anyway, she liked that Tithonus didn't take her goddess status too seriously and mostly treated her as an equal. When she was with him, she could be herself. Even talk occasionally about subjects she usually avoided—like her dad, for example. Because absent fathers were something she and Tithonus had in common. An excellent listener, he was the kind of friend who made her feel, well . . . *lighthearted*!

Speaking of listening, she was suddenly aware that she hadn't been. Tithonus had fallen silent, and she'd missed most of what he'd said about his unusual dragonfly bug.

"You okay?" he asked. "You're all quiet." A lock of his wavy brown hair fell forward as he bent toward her a little. His hair was so unruly that it always looked as if he never combed it. But that was partly the fault of a wayward lock above the center of his forehead.

"Are you saying I'm usually a bigmouth?" Eos teased. Then she giggled and admitted, "Sorry. I just spaced out."

"S'okay," Tithonus said good-naturedly. He smoothed back the lock of hair from his forehead as they continued toward school. Instantly, it sprang out of place again. "Darn hair. I can never get this one piece to lie flat. No matter what I do, it always boings up, like a cow licked it in the wrong direction." He grinned slyly at her, adding, "Which is why it's called a cowlick."

She laughed. Tithonus liked learning about word origins and sort of collected them. But maybe that was because of how much time he had to spend using the dictionary! Writing and spelling were his worst subjects in school.

"Anything new with Nyx?" Tithonus asked, changing the subject. "You saw her this morning, right?"

"Yeah. Hey, that reminds me." Pausing, she opened her schoolbag to take out Nyx's note. She'd expected it to be on top, since it was the last thing she'd put into her bag. Only it wasn't there, so it must have fallen deeper inside. "Nyx gave me a notescroll today," she explained as he waited for her while she rummaged through her bag. "I haven't read it yet."

"No worries," he said, glancing upward. "Guessing from the position of Helios's chariot, we won't be late for school. We're cutting it close, though."

"Really? Sorry." Eos closed her bag and rushed off again. "I can look for the notescroll later. So, unless you stop to look at grasshoppers or some other bugs, we should make it on time."

At her teasing, Tithonus made a face. "Puh-leeze. Grasshoppers are *insects*, not bugs. Although the word 'bugs' is often used as a general category that includes insects, that's technically not correct. Bugs have no teeth, so they suck juices from plants. *Insects* do have teeth, at least sort of. They belong to the class Insecta and have three-part bodies, three pairs of legs, and usually two pairs of wings. Bees are an example of insects, as are—"

"Grasshoppers," Eos supplied as they rounded a corner and started down another street. Whenever he started on the subject of bugs, it was hard to get him to stop. Grasshoppers were currently Tithonus's favorite bug—er, *insect*. Suddenly, without meaning to, she yawned.

"Am I boring you?" he asked. Then he yawned too. "Argh. Stop it. Yawning is catching."

"You're not boring," Eos assured him. "It's just that you know I've got grasshopper brains."

He raised his eyebrows at her, grinning. "Tiny, you mean?"

"Ha-ha." She elbowed him. "No, I mean my attention is always jumping from one thing to another."

She yawned again, and he gave her the stink eye when it made him yawn again too. "Sorry," she told him. "I stayed up late last night studying for my geography quiz today. Then I had to get up before dawn, of course. Not enough sleep."

"Nyx would not approve," he said. They both knew that one of the reasons Nyx loved bringing the night was because it helped people sleep, something she considered very important for everyone's health.

Eos nodded in agreement. Speaking of Nyx, she was really dying to read her notescroll. She opened her bag again and blindly plunged the fingers of one hand deep into her bag, trying to locate the scroll as they walked.

Meanwhile Tithonus shifted his schoolbag to his other hand and kept on talking. "Did you know that when grasshoppers sleep, their body temperature drops to the same temperature as their surroundings, and their heartbeat and breathing slow way down? If they get too cold, their wing muscles can't move fast enough for them to fly."

"Glad I don't have that problem," Eos replied. Her wings had been folded at her sides, but now she fluttered them slightly, which caused her to rise about a foot off the ground. "Otherwise I might have trouble flying out on cold winter mornings to do my job." She refolded her wings so her feet touched down again.

Just as their school came into view up ahead, her fingers curled around something the right shape and size at the bottom of her bag. "Gotcha!" she declared victoriously. She pulled out Nyx's notescroll and held it up.

Tithonus nodded as they quickened their pace.

"Cool! We're almost to school. So are you going to read that scroll to me, or what?"

"Depends. Could be secret girl stuff." She unrolled the short scroll and scanned it. Realizing it didn't contain anything she'd rather keep private, she excitedly read it aloud:

> *Hi Eos,*
>
> *Remember how I told you the unveiling of the new statue of me in Artemis's temple at Ephesus had to be postponed? Because of that storm that damaged the temple? Well, the damage is fixed (yay!) and the unveiling is on again! Can you come to the ceremony? I hope, I hope, I hope? It's tomorrow (Saturday) at 2pm.*
>
> *Your friend,*
>
> *Nyx*

"Cool! Wow! You're going to go, right?" Tithonus asked.

"Maybe," said Eos, tucking away the scroll as they entered the school grounds.

As everyone knew, Artemis was goddess of the hunt, a skilled archer, and a student at Mount Olympus Academy. She had decided to place a statue of Nyx in her temple to honor the goddess of the night's importance to the world. Nyx had gotten to visit MOA after Artemis and another goddessgirl named Athena won a contest for an essay they'd written about Nyx, praising her as an "unsung hero." Once this statue was put in place, Nyx wouldn't be "unsung" any longer. Everyone could celebrate her at the temple!

"Nyx deserves this honor, and I want to be there," added Eos. "But Ephesus is a long way off. It'd take me almost eight hours to fly there—one way. I'd have to set out on the journey right after dawn and start back soon after the ceremony."

"That *is* a long trip," Tithonus sympathized. "Still, if *I* were you, I'd go in a hot second!" Then, as if it were a done deal, he added, "Hey, if you meet Ares, get his autograph for me, will you? Zeus's, too—I once saw his autograph on a tablet in the temple dedicated to him in Athens. He drew a cool thunderbolt next to it." Tithonus did a little skip and punched one fist in the air. "Awesome!"

Gulp. Would Zeus be there? wondered Eos. What if she *did* go and she came face-to-face with him? Would she be able to control that sad-mad feeling about her father? Or would she lash out and draw Zeus's anger? An image of the powerful god filled her mind, and she shuddered. Though she'd never seen him in person, she'd once seen a life-size statue of him. Judging from that, he had to be seven feet tall, with bulging muscles and a stern gaze.

She'd also seen pictures of him in *Greekly Weekly News* and *Teen Scrollazine*. He had wild red hair and bushy eyebrows. And thick golden bracelets that encircled his wrists. Sometimes the pictures showed him in action, tossing thunderbolts across the sky. If she made him mad, would he hurl one her way? Blow her to smithereens?

Eos was jolted back to the present when the school door appeared before her. "We're here already?" she said in surprise. She hadn't even noticed walking that last part to get here!

Tithonus pushed open the door and held it so she could enter first. He was nice that way. Another thing she liked about him. "Thanks," she told him as he followed her inside.

"So? You decide yet? About going to that temple thing?" he went on.

They didn't have a single class together this year, so unless they saw each other in the cafeteria at lunchtime, or in the hallway between classes, this would be their last chance to talk before the end of the day.

She shrugged. Before he could continue "bugging" her about whether or not she would go to the unveiling, two friends of his named Cleitus and Cephalus called his name. Short and round, the identical twin boys had black hair and always dressed in shiny black tunics.

"When's the funeral?" Cleitus yelled.

"Right after school," Tithonus called back. He waved bye to Eos and took a step in the twins' direction.

"What funeral?" Eos called after him in confusion.

Tithonus looked over his shoulder at her. "One of my beetles died." He often kept bugs and insects as pets. "Us guys are having a funeral for it after school. Wanna come?"

"Um . . . oh, wait, I can't," Eos told him, kind of relieved, actually. "I've got track practice and a Scrollbook Club meeting after school today."

"Track practice. Right," Tithonus said while jogging backward. He had admitted to her once that he'd always wished *he* were better at sports, especially since all the other boys seemed to be good at them. And though he truly wished to have track skills, he'd also confessed that he wasn't interested in practicing hard enough to improve. That would take too much time away from his precious bugs!

Unlike Tithonus, Eos not only played on several

sports teams, but she was also president or copresident of four different after-school clubs. She didn't excel at any of these, however. Probably because the time she spent on each activity was limited with so many of them. But that was okay with her. She had fun trying lots of things, and she was good enough at them that she was usually welcomed by others in whatever she did.

"Okay, then. You're missing out, though," said Tithonus, smiling. "Later, Busy Bee!" He turned to meet up with his friends, and the three boys headed off for class together.

As she walked on down the hall, Eos thought about how Tithonus never seemed overly upset about a pet bug's death. Probably because bugs and insects naturally had short life spans. Which meant he was always having funerals for them (complete with small bug caskets decorated with art and silly rhyming poems he made up that celebrated their lives).

Thinking of funerals, a wave of sadness washed over her. Because it had just occurred to her that *Tithonus's* life span was going to be short too. Not as short as a bug's, but way shorter than hers. Since Eos was a goddess, that meant she was immortal and would never face death. Tithonus, though, like all the other students at Oceanus Middle School, was a mortal. He was going to grow old. And then one day he'd die. Of course that was a long way off. But still. Tithonus was her best friend!

If only he were a godboy instead of a mortal prince. Then he'd be immortal just like her. And if he were immortal, they could stay friends forever.

Luckily, before she could really start to worry

about this, a group of friends she knew from clubs, sports, and classes swept her up in their midst. As she continued down the hall, giggling and chatting with them on her way to her first-period class, Eos's heavy heart grew light again.

3
Scrollbook Club

TURNED OUT THAT EOS DIDN'T ACE HER second-period geography quiz, but she was happy enough with her B grade. She finished her first-period math-class assignment during third-period science while the teacher talked about the upcoming science fair to be held next Friday, a week from today. Should she enter? *Hmm. Maybe not.* She had to draw the line with all her activities somewhere!

During a lecture in fifth-period history, she completed a short essay on Homer for her fourth-period language-arts class. They'd been studying Homer's epic poems *The Iliad* and *The Odyssey* in class. By the end of the day, she'd done all her homework. Score! Since she was involved in so many activities, she had learned to be efficient with her time.

Once school was out, she headed for track-team practice out on the sports field. Ms. Megalos was a great coach. Even though Eos wasn't the fastest runner on the team by far, she'd improved a lot under the coach's direction. After practice, a quick shower, and a change of clothes in the locker room, she used her track skills to sprint to the library for Scrollbook Club!

Winging it, or even vaporizing herself for travel (something she could do for short periods of time), would have gotten her to the library faster. However, after an unfortunate incident a few years ago, she'd made it a rule never to do either of those things at school ever again. In fact, she kept her wings folded tight at her sides at all times around here. This helped minimize the differences between her and the mortals, making it easier to fit in.

Unfortunately, although she could control her wings, she couldn't help that her skin shimmered lightly, marking her as an immortal. And she couldn't keep the pink vapory mist that floated from her fingertips from occasionally seeping out. The mist always faded quickly into the air, but these things set her apart from the other kids at her school and made them sometimes stare and whisper.

She put this small problem out of her mind as she entered the library for Scrollbook Club. Not only was she the president, but she was also the founder of the club. It had fifteen members, mostly girls, and met once a month to discuss a scrollbook they'd agreed to read the previous month. Not everyone came to every meeting, but at least half the group came each time. And though anyone could suggest what to read, more often than not the members let Eos decide. She hoped it was because they liked her suggestions, and not because she was the club's founder and president. (Or worse, because she was a goddess!)

"So who all finished the scrollbook this time?" Eos asked, looking around at the girls seated in the circle of chairs that had been set up for the meeting. This month's scrollbook was *Callirhoe*, by Chariton of Aphrodisias. Eos had suggested the scrollbook because, though she knew the romance part of the story might not appeal to the boys in the club, there were pirates, and enough action in the plot that both boys and girls might enjoy it.

Apparently she hadn't been successful at convincing the boys to overlook the romantic aspect. While nine other girls had made it to the meeting, no boys had. Oh well. Everyone had different tastes. It was hard to pick a scrollbook that everyone liked!

Only three hands besides her own had gone up to indicate they'd read the scrollbook. Eos was unable to stop herself from saying, "Great, but what about the rest of you?" At recent meetings, it seemed that fewer and fewer members had actually read the month's selection. And, truthfully, this had begun to bug her a little. Well, a lot, really. Because if *she* was able to finish each scrollbook with her busy schedule, surely others could too.

With guilty expressions on their faces, the six slackers looked down at their laps. After a few seconds of awkward silence, a girl named Agatha looked up. "I had too much homework to finish it."

"I see," said Eos, tapping her fingertips on the table in irritation. Before she could stop herself, she added, "I had a lot of homework this month too. Plus, as you all know, I have to get up very early each morning." Usually she avoided references to her dawn-bringing job since it was another reminder of how different she was from these mortals, but she was so annoyed that the comment just slipped out.

Agatha's face turned pale. "S-sorry," she stammered. "I'll try to do better n-next time."

Ye gods, thought Eos. You'd think the girl was afraid of her. Was she? Did she think Eos might lose her temper and smite her or something? No way!

"Hey, I'm not mad. It's okay," Eos assured Agatha and the other five non-finishers, who'd also begun to look a little nervous. "Maybe our discussion will inspire you to read the rest of the scrollbook later." Swallowing her annoyance, she smiled brightly to show that she meant none of them any harm. If only everyone at school would relax around her like Tithonus did.

"And maybe not," quipped Zoe, one of the other non-finishers. This prompted nervous giggles from the group. Zoe and Agatha were best friends, and Eos knew Zoe probably wasn't happy she had upset Agatha just now.

"So you didn't like the story?" Eos asked Zoe.

Zoe shrugged. "I couldn't get into it. I like *true* stories."

"Okay," Eos said agreeably. Then, in an encouraging tone, she asked, "Would you like to suggest one to read for our next meeting?"

"Um. I'm not good at remembering titles," Zoe mumbled.

Eos sighed. Looking around at the other girls, she said, "Shall we go ahead and discuss this month's scrollbook?" She couldn't resist adding, "Those of us who actually read it?"

To her dismay, Agatha burst into tears. "Don't be so mean. We're mortals. We can't all be p-perfect like you. We don't have m-magic!"

Eos's face fell. She hadn't meant to make Agatha cry. But before she could apologize, Zoe, angry on behalf of her friend, blurted out, "I know! Next time, let's read about the war between the Olympians and the Titans. Who doesn't like a true story about good versus *evil*?"

Everyone gasped, looking between Zoe and Eos with big eyes. As the whole school knew, Eos's father was a Titan god. Yes, he'd been on the losing side of the war, and yes, her feelings about him were complicated. But that didn't give anyone the right to call him *evil*!

In an instant, Eos completely lost it. *Whoosh!* She unfurled her wings. A terrified silence fell over the room, as she flapped them and rose to hover menacingly over Zoe.

Fortunately, before she could do anything worse than just hover, some small part of her brain realized she'd broken her own rule. *Stop! Think what you're doing!* it silently yelled out. She took a deep breath to calm herself, then fluttered back down to her chair and refolded her wings.

"Sorry," she said to the room at large, though she

couldn't quite bring herself to meet anyone's eyes. She hadn't flapped her wings in school since second grade! Hadn't she learned her lesson back then?

"Maybe, instead of talking about the story today— since only a few of us have read it—we could talk about something else?" one of the girls suggested. "If that's okay with you, Eos?" she added uncertainly.

Though Eos wanted to protest that the whole purpose of the club was to talk about scrollbooks, she nodded. "Okay. What do you want to talk about?" She did not want these girls to think they had no say in what the group did. Or to fear her anger if they didn't do what she wanted.

Someone took out the latest issue of *Teen Scrollazine*. As the girls began to chat about the articles in it, they grew more enthusiastic and less scared-looking. "Ooh, did you see the article about

Orion?" remarked a girl named Jacinta. "I got to see him in a play once. He's so cute, and he has the best smile!"

"Orion the dreamy teen actor?" asked Zoe.

He was a megastar, Eos knew. The mortal boy had won lots of acting prizes and had even had a constellation named after him! Although he was good-looking and popular, she had heard he was quite full of himself.

"Yeah, there's an interview in this issue with him talking about all his successes," said Jacinta.

"He doesn't have many good things to say about the other actors he's worked with," Agatha noted. "He says a lot of them tried to hold him back."

Eos rolled her eyes. Well, at least they were discussing *something* written, even if it was a 'zine instead of a scrollbook. However, she didn't join in as most of the other girls gushed about Orion. Instead she mulled over what had just happened with Zoe. Not since that event in second grade had prompted her to make a no-flying-at-school rule had anyone dared mention the Titans or her dad to her.

Back then, a girl named Nefili (which meant "cloud," a word that fit the girl's dark and cloudy personality perfectly) had made a cutting remark about Eos's dad and how he "got what he deserved" in the war. Eos had flown into a rage. Flapping her wings wildly, she'd plucked Nefili from her chair in the classroom and risen up to the ceiling, threatening to drop her.

She could still recall how Nefili had screamed, "I'm sorry! I'm sorry!" And she could still see in her mind the horrified faces of the other students who'd observed all this from below. Still hear their gasps of fear. Their terror had broken her anger, and she'd fluttered back down. As soon as they hit solid ground, Nefili, though unharmed, had burst into tears and raced from the room.

Eos had gotten in trouble, of course. The kind that meant a visit to the principal's office and worse. Even at that young age, she'd figured she deserved it. She'd known that mortals could not only get hurt; they could actually die. Though her threat had been a bluff, and she wouldn't have dropped the wiggly girl on purpose, she might have done it accidentally.

As punishment for her actions, she'd spent every lunchtime and recess for the following two weeks in the principal's office. Even worse, Tithonus's mom hadn't allowed them to play together until she felt she could trust Eos again. It had been a horrible time!

After that, Eos and her mom had made a plan for keeping what had happened from ever happening again. It had been Eos's own idea to make it a rule never to fly at school. A rule that had the added benefit of making her seem less different from other students. And she'd made a promise to herself to never harm a friend (or even a foe) again. Had she blown it today, with this one lapse?

She glanced sideways at Zoe. Catching the girl's eye, she did her best to smile. After a moment's hesitation, Zoe gave her a half smile in return. Eos dared to hope this little episode wouldn't become legend, the way the one with Nefili had. The story of what had happened with that girl was probably one of the first things new students heard about when they started at Oceanus Middle School!

But whatever gossip this episode with Zoe might

inspire, deep down Eos knew that, despite all her efforts to blend in here and to participate in as many school activities as possible, the other students would always remain cautious around her. Even as they befriended her and played with her on teams and joined her clubs. And knowing this made her feel like an outsider.

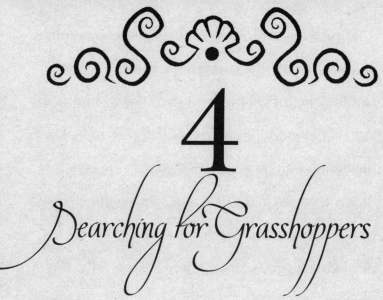

4

Searching for Grasshoppers

Eos WAS RELIEVED WHEN SCROLLBOOK CLUB finally ended. She quickly scooted out of the library and through the school's front doors. Only when the school building was no longer in sight and no students were around did she unfurl her wings and fly toward home. A thrilling feeling of freedom washed over her once she was airborne. And the lightheartedness she'd felt that morning returned.

From the sky she spied Tithonus roaming around in a field of tall grass behind his home. Every now and then he cocked his ear toward the ground as if listening intently and bent over the grass to look at something with his magnifying glass.

Eos set down in the field instead of continuing on to her house. Dropping her schoolbag, she waded through the grass toward him. "Hey, Bug Boy. Funeral over?"

Tithonus jumped in surprise. "Yeah. Where'd you come from, Busy Bee?"

"I *spi*dered you from the air," she joked. "Looking for insects?" It was a reasonable guess.

He grinned at her joke and nodded, causing his cowlick to flop forward. "Yeah, which means I'm not looking for spiders. They're arachnids, not insects, ya know."

She grinned back. "Yeah, I know. Eight legs instead of six, blah, blah," she teased. He'd told her all kinds of stuff about spiders before.

"I'm looking for grasshoppers." He smoothed back the wayward lock of hair, and his eyes darted to the field again. "They feed here. Sometimes you can hear the chirping sound they make when they rub their hind legs against their wings."

Eos noticed that he was holding a glass jar with a wide mouth. "Is that going to be your new pet's home?"

"Yeah." He held up the jar so she could see it better. "After I capture it, I'll be able to observe it up close."

They walked through the grass for a minute or two, and then suddenly Tithonus stopped. "There's one," he whispered, pointing to a grasshopper clinging to a blade of grass. "See it?"

Eos nodded. The grasshopper was green with brown spots. Its short antennae quivered as Tithonus approached it. He moved slowly, till he was within arm's reach of the insect. But as he moved to place the jar over the top of the grasshopper, it hopped away.

"Oh, too bad," Eos said. "That little guy was fast!"

"Yeah. Its oversize hind legs allow it to jump long distances." Tithonus's eyes searched for the insect but didn't find it. "I'll look for another one. And maybe try using my hands next time."

It wasn't long before they spied another grass-hopper feeding on a stalk of grass. "Hold the jar for me," Tithonus whispered. Eos took it from him, nodding.

Like the first grasshopper, this one had a large head connected to a long, sturdy-looking body. "That one's even bigger than the first one," Eos whispered as she cradled the jar. "Hey, why are we whispering? Can grasshoppers hear?"

"Yeah," Tithonus murmured. "But not with ears. They hear through an organ called a tympanum at the base of their hind legs." He moved closer to the new prospect. "This one's probably a female. They're bigger than the males." Once again he approached the grasshopper slowly. His magnifying glass dangled from his belt. Grasshoppers were large enough to be plenty visible without it.

This time Tithonus kept his hands out in front of him, holding one on either side of the grass-hopper. Then, before it could notice what he was doing and hop away, Tithonus quickly brought his hands together, trapping the insect between cupped palms. "Gotcha!"

"Pink!" Eos cried out in delight. While she held

out the jar, he transferred the grasshopper into it. To keep it from hopping right back out, he took a piece of loosely woven cloth from the pocket of his tunic. After laying it across the top of the jar, he fished a piece of string from his pocket and tied the cloth scrap around the neck of the jar.

"Um, is that insect poop?" Eos asked, pointing to a wet-looking brown stain on one of Tithonus's hands.

He shrugged. "When grasshoppers feel threat-ened, they release a brown liquid. Perfectly harmless."

"Ugh." Eos wrinkled her nose. "I mean, you know I don't mind bugs and insects, but . . . no. That's just . . . no."

Tithonus laughed. "You get used to it." Bending down, he rubbed his hand on the grass to get rid of the stain.

Shaking her head, Eos declared, "*I* wouldn't! I'm okay with insects and all, but that's just plain *gross*-hopper!"

They both laughed. Before they started back across the field, Tithonus picked some fresh-looking grass shoots. Carefully lifting one edge of the cloth, he slid the shoots inside the jar. "So Melody will have something to eat," he explained.

Eos lifted an eyebrow as she handed him the jar to carry. "Melody?"

Tithonus grinned. "Good name, huh? I chose it because of the chirping sound grasshoppers make. Look at her munching away already." Without looking up from the jar, he said, "Hey, you missed a good funeral today. The twins came up with some killer rhymes and songs."

"Yeah, sorry I missed it," she said. And she really

was. Track practice had been fine, but Scrollbook Club had been a disaster! She would have gladly attended the bug funeral instead. As they started back through the field, she added, "How long do grasshoppers live, anyway?"

"Out here in the wild, only for a couple of months," Tithonus told her. "Cold weather can kill them. And they get eaten by spiders, birds, snakes, and rodents. Cats, too," he added as his pet cat, a calico he'd named Bugs, came toward them through the grass.

"Wow, that's not very long," mused Eos. She stooped to pet Bugs. But the cat—a girl, like most calicos—spotted something interesting across the field and soon scampered away.

Tithonus shrugged. "Probably seems that way to you, especially since you're immortal. But from a grasshopper's point of view, maybe that's a long time. Anyway, Melody could actually live for a year or more, since I'll be keeping her in a warm, safe jar."

"I'm glad," said Eos. She stared at him as he studied his bug—er, *insect.* Tithonus likely thought the life span of mortals was a long time. Compared to the life span of insects and bugs, it really was. But, as had occurred to her in the school hallway only that morning, a mortal life span was super short compared to an immortal's. And, just as it had before, a wave of sadness swept over her at the thought. Someone as awesome as Tithonus should live forever!

"I wish I could make more people care about insects," he said, breaking up her melancholy thoughts. "They're so important to the environment. And so interesting, too. They're way underappreciated."

Spotting the schoolbag she'd dropped upon landing, Eos dashed a short distance away to retrieve it. As she bounded back, she thought about what Tithonus had said. The upcoming science fair suddenly flashed into her head.

She snapped her fingers. "I just had the greatest idea, Tithonus! Why don't you do a science fair exhibit about Melody with all kinds of information about grasshoppers!"

Tithonus's brown eyes lit up. But then he frowned. "I don't know. It's next Friday, right?"

Eos nodded. "A week from today."

Tithonus rubbed the back of his neck. "That's not a lot of time, especially for the writing part. . . ."

Eos could've kicked herself for momentarily blanking on the fact that Tithonus had trouble with writing and spelling. He was so mega-smart in other ways that it was easy to forget.

"I'll help you," she said quickly. "You can tell me what you want to say, and I'll organize it and write it all down."

"Really?" His brown eyes lit up again. "I can make the diagrams and sketches," he said with growing enthusiasm.

"Perfect! You're great at that stuff," Eos said. Which was true. Tithonus was mega-good at drawing. "We can get most of it done over the weekend."

"What about Nyx's statue unveiling tomorrow, though?" Tithonus glanced over at her as they left the field and walked toward her house. "You're going, right?"

"Well, I don't *have* to," Eos replied. "Ephesus is so far away. She'll understand if I can't make it." At least she *hoped* Nyx would understand. Besides, Eos hadn't even asked her mom about going.

Not that her mom would say no. It wasn't as if the two of them had plans to do anything together this weekend. Which was okay. Only there were times lately when she kind of missed her mom. Too bad they couldn't spend more time together. But Eos was busy with school and clubs. And her mom had her hobbies and volunteer efforts for various charities, plus weekly visits to the Underworld (which Eos *never* joined her on).

"You should go," Tithonus urged. "You'd have fun. Plus, you could be around other goddessgirls and godboys for a change. While you're gone, I can think about what I want you to help me write and start on my drawings and sketches. We can work on the science fair project Sunday."

Eos looked at him in surprise. Had he guessed that she often felt like an outsider, being the only immortal at school and in their neighborhood? Maybe she *should* go to Ephesus. She wanted to support Nyx. And hang out with her too, since that was something she never really got the chance to do. There would probably be so many gods and goddesses at the unveiling that she could easily avoid Zeus—*if* he even came.

"Yeah. You're right," she told Tithonus, just before she split off from him to head into her house. "I'll go if Mom says I can."

That night, when Eos asked for permission to go to the unveiling, her mother barely looked up as she nodded her approval. She and some other ladies she'd invited over were busy putting together care packages for mortals affected by a recent earthquake on the Greek island of Crete.

"Ephesus is a long way to go," Eos reminded her mom. "I would be back really late."

"That's fine," Theia said distractedly.

Ye gods! Eos knew she should be glad her mother trusted her to go on such a long journey alone. But couldn't she show a little more concern? Moms were *supposed* to worry about their kids. It was proof they cared deeply about them!

"Take your cloak, though. It could get chilly," Theia added.

"Okay, I will," said Eos as she headed for her room. That was a little more like it. Still, she wouldn't have minded if her mom acted a bit more, well, mom-ish sometimes. Like Tithonus's mom, who was always in his business and totally focused on taking care of him.

Eos made her way through the house to the center of the courtyard. After vaporizing herself, she corkscrew-dove into her urn-room with a whoosh. Then she quickly donned her favorite striped orange-and-pink pj's. Since she'd done all her homework at school, she grabbed some old issues of *Teen Scrollazine* and plopped onto her bed with them. Though she figured she wouldn't have much trouble recognizing the various goddessgirls and godboys she'd see at Nyx's unveiling tomorrow, she leafed through the pictures in the 'zines anyway, just to refresh her memory.

She smiled to herself as she snuggled down in her covers a little later, thinking about hunting for grass-hoppers that day with Tithonus. Bugs—er, insects—were interesting. But mostly it was just hanging out with him that made things fun!

Suddenly her lighthearted thoughts turned dark.

Someday when Tithonus was old and she was still young, he wouldn't want to hang out with her and do stuff like bug hunting anymore. That would be so *not* fair! If she and Nyx could stay young and live forever, why shouldn't he?

She rolled onto her side thinking of how she'd be meeting lots of goddessgirls and godboys from MOA at tomorrow's unveiling. Hey! Maybe one of them knew a way to make Tithonus immortal. And maybe they'd tell *her* how to do it!

5

The Temple of Artemis

WHEN EOS ARRIVED AT HER USUAL SPOT IN the sky Saturday morning, ready to bring forth the dawn, she looked up at Nyx and waved the notescroll her friend had given her. "Yes! I can come see your statue!" she shouted.

Nyx flashed Eos a smile, already reeling in her cape. "Hooray!" she whooped. "I'm going home to sleep for a few hours and then Hades will give me a ride to the temple at Ephesus. He's got four stallions to pull his chariot, which means his can go much faster than mine!"

At the mention of Hades, Eos paled. A student at MOA, he was also godboy of the Underworld, where Nyx lived, and where mortals like Tithonus would go when they died. It was also where some unlucky immortals were imprisoned right now—those who had fought against Zeus in battle or defied him in some other way. As a matter of fact, her sad-mad-dad problem was *all* tied into the Underworld. Because one of those immortal prisoners was her dad, Hyperion, the god of light!

"Hey! Eos! The dawn?" With a start, Eos realized Nyx had finished reeling in her entire cape and was ready to ride away.

Oops! Swallowing the sudden lump that had come

into her throat at the thought of her dad, Eos went into action. She had a job to do! Quickly, she raised both arms over her head. Concentrating on her work, she flicked her wrists and sent her glistening rays of pink, purple, and orange toward the horizon.

"See you this afternoon!" she called out as Nyx swept past in her chariot, taking the night with her.

Nyx smiled down at her. "Yeah! Can't wait!"

About a half hour later, job done, Eos set off for Ephesus. She had brought a backpack with snacks, a lunch, and the cloak her mom had advised her to bring. She planned to take breaks whenever she grew tired of flying. Even with the breaks, she was pretty sure she could make it to the celebration on time.

Pumping her feathery white wings, she rose high over land, trees, and rivers to head farther east.

Now that she had an additional big reason to go to the unveiling—namely, to discover a way to make Tithonus immortal—she was very glad he had convinced her to attend.

She made her way over the Aegean Sea between Greece and Asia Minor, switching back and forth between wing travel and vapor travel. The breezes blowing up from the sea were chilly. Halfway over the sea, she pulled the cloak out of her backpack and put it on, glad her mom had reminded her to bring it.

Once Eos had crossed the Aegean, she soon spied Troy in Asia Minor—Tithonus's birthplace. Sometime before the famous Trojan War had been fought here, he had lost his father, brothers, and a sister to a terrible plague. Probably to get away from unhappy memories, his mom had moved Tithonus and herself to the other side of the Aegean.

Tithonus himself had no memories of that dark time, he'd told Eos once. He'd been a toddler when they'd moved. About the same age she had been the last time she'd seen her dad.

Eos let her wings take her lower to land in Troy. Then she sat on a large boulder and took her lunch out of her backpack. As she munched her sandwich, she reflected on how, whenever she felt sorry for herself that her father was a prisoner in the Underworld, she had only to remind herself of Tithonus's losses. Things could be much worse for her, she realized. Though she couldn't bring herself to visit her dad in the Underworld, at least she knew he was still alive.

Taking to the air again, Eos banished thoughts of him and continued winging and vaporizing her way south, approaching Ephesus at last. She gasped in awe when Artemis's temple came into view. It was gigantic! Rectangular in shape and built of gleaming white marble, it was surrounded by columns on all four sides.

Eos touched down a short distance from the steps that led up to the temple and folded her wings. Several Mount Olympus Academy chariots were parked nearby, each bearing an MOA logo with a thunderbolt emblazoned on their sides. A quick peek at a sundial showed that it was a little before two in the afternoon. Yay! She'd made it here on time!

As she moved toward the temple, Eos gazed up at it. It was even more impressive viewed from the ground than from up in the air. Its columns, many of them decorated by carvings in relief, had to be at least forty feet high! And even more carvings adorned the triangular area under its peaked roof.

She spotted several goddessgirls and godboys she recognized from *Teen Scrollazine* and the *Greekly Weekly News* milling around. Though excited that she would be among so many fellow immortals, Eos slowed her steps, suddenly feeling a bit shy and unsure of herself. Then she saw Nyx arrive with the dark-haired, serious-faced Hades and a goddessgirl with pale skin and long red curls. She was Persephone, the goddessgirl of growing things and also Hades's crush. Regaining her confidence, Eos rushed forward, waving.

Nyx saw her at once. "Eos!" she shouted joyfully. "Come meet Hades and Persephone!"

Eos ran over to hug Nyx, and then turned toward Persephone. "Hi," she said.

"Nyx told us you'd be coming. So nice to meet

you!" Persephone said by way of greeting. Then she smiled big.

Eos smiled back. "Yeah. You, too." She greeted Hades as well, though a bit warily since he was god-boy of the Underworld. Did he know her father? Probably, but she didn't ask. Sometimes she wondered if more people besides Zoe thought her dad was bad . . . or even *evil*. Maybe he was! How would she know? Except for the daybreak-delight sandwiches he had made for her, her memories of him were hazy at best. Oh, it was all too confusing! So, as usual, she pushed away thoughts of her sad-mad-dad problem.

"Look! Aphrodite and Athena are here!" Nyx called out excitedly. She pointed toward a silver chariot that had just landed. It had pink seats and was hitched to three silver reindeer. Eos easily recognized the two newcomers as they stepped down from their chariot.

Athena was the one with long wavy brown hair, wearing a light blue chiton. She was the goddessgirl of wisdom, Zeus's daughter, and of course she had coauthored the essay about Nyx that had led to today's celebration. Aphrodite, the goddessgirl of love and beauty, was dressed in a sparkly (and *very* fashion-forward) pink chiton.

"Nyx!" Aphrodite squealed, spotting her alongside Eos, Persephone, and Hades at the bottom of the temple steps. As she and Athena ran toward the group, Aphrodite's long golden hair, threaded with pale pink ribbons, streamed out behind her. Several boys nearby turned to look at her with love-struck gazes. That was the kind of response the goddessgirl of love and beauty inspired!

Aphrodite barely noticed all the attention as she caught Nyx up in a big hug. Athena hugged her too. Afterward, Nyx introduced them both to Eos.

"You're goddessgirl of the dawn, aren't you?" asked Athena. Eos nodded, pleased that Athena knew her goddess title. Then Aphrodite clasped her hands together and said with enthusiasm, "I love the dawn—whenever I'm up in time to see it. Those colors you create are spectacular! Especially love all those pinks!" There were murmurs of agreement from the others.

Eos glowed with pleasure. These immortals were so nice! She noticed that, unlike her mortal friends, they all had skin that shimmered slightly like hers. Here she wasn't so different. No one eyed her wings. And whenever colorful vapor drifted out from her fingertips to form a mist in the air, no one stared in surprise. They were used to magic. She felt herself relax.

Nyx was beside Eos as the group began to move into the temple. "I want you to meet Artemis, too," she told Eos.

Overhearing, Athena said, "She's probably inside already. She came early to make sure everything was set up the way she wanted."

Once inside the temple, Eos barely had time to glance at all the statues lining its walls, including an ebony one of Artemis sculpted from grape wood, before she was introduced to even more goddessgirls and godboys. All were Olympians, and had been the enemies of her Titan family during the war. Though she wasn't exactly sure what she'd expected—given that *some* of them must have known who her father was—they were all super welcoming.

Encouraged by their friendliness, Eos asked Athena, in as casual a tone as she could manage, "Will your dad be here for the unveiling?"

Athena shook her head. "He couldn't come. Something about a tournament he was playing in. Not sure what kind of tournament, though."

Maybe a thunderbolt-throwing one? Eos immediately thought. But that couldn't be it. Who else besides Zeus could even throw a thunderbolt? Anyway, it was a huge relief that he wasn't going to show up here.

"Waa! Waaa!"

Eos startled as loud cries split the air. She turned and saw a statuesque blond-haired woman carrying a bundle of blankets into the temple. Inside those blankets was a crying baby.

"That's my stepmom, Hera," Athena informed

Eos. "And the little noisemaker in her arms is my baby sister, Hebe," she added with a smile.

"So I guessed," Eos told her, having read about Hebe in her scrollazine last night. "Is it fun having a baby sister? My sister and brother are older than me, so I wouldn't know."

Athena cocked her head and thought about it. "Well, I didn't much like being a big sister at first," she admitted. "But now I *love* it. Hebe's so adorable and cute and fun and—"

"Hooray! The guest of honor has arrived!" someone cheered, causing Athena to break off mid-sentence. The person who had shouted was a goddessgirl dressed in red with a quiver of arrows and an archery bow slung over her shoulders. Artemis, of course. Her eyes were fixed on Nyx as she hurried toward Eos's group.

As in pictures Eos had seen in *Teen Scrollazine*, Artemis's glossy black hair was caught up in a cute, simple twist high at the back of her head and encircled by golden bands. She was accompanied by three dogs, which ran ahead of her and leaped all over Nyx as soon as they reached her.

"Obviously they remember you from your visit to MOA, Nyx," Artemis said, looking flushed and excited about today's festivities. After gently scolding her dogs, she gave Nyx a hug.

"I didn't know dogs were allowed in temples," Eos murmured to Athena.

"They're not, usually," replied a godboy standing near them. "But since this temple is dedicated to my sister, she can make her own rules!"

"You're Apollo!" Eos exclaimed. She'd seen his picture in the *Greekly Weekly News* and *Teen Scrollazine* many times. Plus, he and his twin sister looked a lot alike.

"You got it," he said. "Eos, right? Nyx wrote my sister that she'd invited you. Cool that you could come."

"Yeah, welcome to my temple!" said Artemis.

"Thanks," Eos told them both. She smiled at Artemis and Apollo, feeling gladder and gladder that Tithonus had urged her to come. Artemis's dogs—curious to meet a stranger, no doubt—trotted up to her to sniff at her hands and chiton. Looking at Artemis, Eos added, "I've never been to Ephesus before. This is the first time I've seen your temple. It's sooo beautiful!"

"Isn't it?" Artemis introduced her dogs to Eos. When Amby, the beagle, rolled over on his back at Eos's feet, she kneeled to scratch his belly.

Artemis grinned. "Belly rubs. He'll be your friend for life now." She laughed, and then glanced over at Apollo. "This is a great turnout!" she enthused, motioning around at all the people who had come.

Apollo grinned back at her. "Didn't I tell you? I predicted it would be a great day."

Artemis giggled. "My brother is good at predictions," she explained to Eos. "Well, *prophecies*, actually. He even prophesied that this temple would be built!"

Eos knew that Apollo was the godboy of truth and prophecy (among other things), but it was still *pink* that he'd foreseen this temple. She glanced at him, intrigued. "How do you get prophecies, anyway? Do you see a picture in your head or hear voices or what?"

Apollo shrugged. "They come in different ways, different times," he said vaguely. "I received the prophecy about Artemis's temple right after I won my own temple—in Delphi."

"Yeah! I remember reading an article about your Delphi temple in *Teen Scrollazine*. You won it in a contest by matching wits with a python! So amazing." Eos started to get excited. Could Apollo predict if—or how—she might succeed in making Tithonus immortal. Eagerly, she asked, "So can you summon a prophecy? Or do you just have to wait for—"

But before she could finish asking her questions, two godboys called to Apollo from across the temple. She recognized the one with grape leaves tucked in his curly hair as Dionysus, while the blond-haired boy with turquoise eyes and light turquoise skin was Poseidon, godboy of the sea.

"Sorry, gotta go," Apollo said to her. "My band's going to play after the unveiling, and we need to set up." Murmuring a good-bye, he loped over to them.

Watching him go, Eos swallowed her disappointment. Maybe she could catch him later, before she left for home. She'd better not stay too long, though. Even if she left in two hours, it would probably be midnight before she got home. And, as usual, she'd have to be up early tomorrow.

At the sound of a harp, the ceremony began. The crowd moved to stand before a cloth-veiled statue. With Nyx beside her and facing the crowd, Artemis gave a short speech about the events that had led to her decision to seek Zeus's permission to place a statue of Nyx in her temple. Then, as magical fireworks burst overhead, Artemis drew a silver arrow from her quiver. She fit it into her golden bow and *shot* the cloth off the statue!

"Wow! Talk about dramatic," Eos murmured to herself.

As the arrow carried the cloth to the floor, there were cheers of appreciation for the intricate bronze statue, which was actually more of a *statuette*. Less than a foot high, it stood atop a tall pedestal. The statuette showed Nyx in motion floating down from the sky to Earth. Her cape billowed up behind her head, and her toes were pointed in readiness to land. In her right hand she clutched something that looked like a small urn. Eos guessed it was supposed to represent the urn that had briefly held the Oneiroi, three dream spirits that had caused mischief at MOA until Nyx had figured out a clever way to trap them.

Artemis gave another short speech at this point, praising Nyx for her valuable work as goddess of the night. When she had finished, Nyx said a few words of thanks for the honor. Then, after the crowd applauded and cheered, everyone dug into snacks and sweets that had been placed on small tables scattered around the room. Apollo's band, Heavens Above, had set up at one side of the temple, and now they began to play.

Eos watched as Apollo plucked at his kithara, a seven-stringed lyre, and Dionysus blew on his double-reeded aulos, a type of flute. Poseidon was on drums. And Ares, the godboy of war—as well as Aphrodite's crush (you could learn a lot reading *Teen Scrollazine*!)—was the band's singer. Eos found herself tapping her toes along to the music as other guests began to dance. The band was awesome. And Ares had a fantastic voice.

"Come on! Join in!" Aphrodite called to her.

Grabbing Eos's hand, the goddessgirl of love and beauty pulled her onto the makeshift dance floor in front of the band. Nyx was already dancing. She grabbed Eos's other hand, and the three girls twirled each other around and around, laughing when they got dizzy and almost fell down. *Pink!*

Remembering that Tithonus had asked her to get Ares' autograph if he was at the unveiling (Zeus's, too, but luckily Zeus wasn't here), Eos went over to ask him for it when the band took a break. "It's for a friend of mine," she told him. "He's a big fan."

"Sure. No problem," said Ares. "Got a piece of papyrus and a pen?"

"Just a minute." Eos sprinted over to a bench where she'd left her backpack. As she grabbed it, and then raced over to Ares with it, she saw Aphrodite frowning at her. She hoped the goddessgirl didn't think she was flirting with Ares or something. She'd *never* flirt with someone else's crush. Duh. No way was she even interested in *having* a crush.

Locating a feather pen and a piece of blank papyrus at the bottom of her pack, she handed them to Ares. "What's your friend's name?" he asked.

"Tithonus," Eos told him, spelling it for him. "I like your singing," she added as he scribbled a note to Tithonus and signed his name under it. "The band is great. It's been so fun to get to hear you all."

"Thanks." Ares smiled at her as he handed her the autographed note and pen. "Hope you enjoy our next set," he told her. "We start again in just a few minutes."

"Wish I could stay," Eos said. "But I'll need to leave soon since it's a long way home for me. Thanks for the autograph, though. Tithonus will go *buggy* over it!"

When Ares quirked an eyebrow at that last, Eos laughed. "Sorry. Inside joke. Tithonus is a bug expert. He studies all kinds of insects. And sometimes I help him." Spotting Apollo in the entry to the temple, she said a hurried good-bye to Ares.

After tucking the autographed note into her backpack, she slung the pack over one shoulder and started toward Apollo. She'd decided to ask him if he could summon a prophecy to find out if she could successfully make Tithonus immortal.

But before she could reach him, Nyx stopped her. Breaking off a conversation she'd been having with Athena, Nyx eyed Eos's backpack. "You're not leaving already, are you?" she asked anxiously.

"I am," Eos told her and Athena. "I had so much

fun, though. I really appreciate being invited."

"But the party is still going on," Nyx protested.

"I've got a long way to go," Eos reminded her gently. "It'll take me eight hours to get home."

Athena blinked. "Oh no! And I bet you're still tired from the trip over here too, right?"

"I am a bit," Eos admitted. "But I'll be fine."

Athena's forehead wrinkled in thought. A few seconds passed before she said, "I know! Someone could take you back in a chariot instead. Still, that would take a long time too, and—wait a minute!" she exclaimed, interrupting herself. "Why don't you just spend the night at MOA?"

"Yes! Yes! You must!" Nyx enthused. "Then we can all celebrate awhile longer."

Eos hesitated. It *would* be fun to stay longer. She'd been having a great time chatting with other immortals and dancing to Heavens Above's music. Besides, Nyx really wanted her here, and she wanted to support her friend.

"But wouldn't I need an invitation from your dad to sleep over?" she asked Athena. She'd heard that even short stays at MOA required Zeus's approval.

Before Athena could answer, Hera, who had approached so quietly that the girls hadn't noticed her, spoke up. "I can speak for my husband, and of course you must stay," she told Eos firmly. Hebe, who was sleeping with her head against one of Hera's shoulders, stirred a little then. Hera cooed to the baby and swayed from side to side to rock her back to sleep while Athena gave the baby gentle pats and rubs through the blankets.

"So you'll stay?" Nyx asked Eos eagerly while Hera was busy with Hebe. Rushing on before Eos could reply, she added, "C'mon, do it. You'll *love* MOA, I promise. And that will give us more time to see each other, since I won't have to leave to bring night till around seven."

"Well, I . . ." Eos paused, thinking. She could send her colorful rays from anywhere in the sky, including from MOA, so that was not an issue. Already she could hear the band tuning up for their second set of songs. If she left for home now, she'd miss her chance to talk to Apollo. But what if she ran into Zeus while spending the night at MOA? She could *not* let that happen.

"Um, so when does Zeus get back from his tournament?" she asked Athena, trying to sound casual.

Athena shrugged. "Not sure." She cocked her head at Eos. "Did you want to see him about something?"

"No!" Eos said quickly. "But if it's really okay," she added to cover her outburst, "I think I *would* like to spend the night at MOA. Only, my mom—"

Before she could finish explaining that her mom expected her back tonight, Hera interrupted. Hebe was sound asleep against her shoulder again. "Don't worry," she told Eos. "I'll write a messagescroll and have it delivered to let Theia know you'll be spending the night with the girls at MOA."

Eos was surprised that Hera knew her mom's name. But she supposed, since both were goddesses, it made sense. They'd probably met at one time or another. She smiled at Hera. "Okay, thanks!" Now that the decision had been made, she found herself looking forward to staying longer. Although she liked her school well enough, hanging out with Nyx and other immortals really was a special treat.

Hera carefully transferred the sleeping Hebe to Athena's shoulder and then produced a sheet of papyrus and a feather pen from a voluminous white diaper bag decorated with large green dots. No, not dots, Eos realized. *Heads of lettuce!* Oh yeah! She remembered hearing that Athena's little sister had been born from a big ball of lettuce that had magically split open. And in fact, Hebe was also the name of a kind of lettuce.

As Hera dashed off a note to Eos's mom, the band began to play again. Out on the dance floor, Artemis waved to them all. "C'mon!"

"Go on. I'll catch up in a few," Athena told Nyx and Eos. She kissed the top of Hebe's head as she cradled the sleeping baby.

Aww, how sweet, thought Eos. It was easy to see that Athena really did love her baby sister.

It was nearly half past five when the party finally wound down. Since Eos still hadn't found a chance to talk to Apollo, she would just have to catch him at MOA somehow.

She joined Athena and Aphrodite in their silver school chariot to fly back to MOA. Athena and Aphrodite sat on the pink bench up front, while Eos sat in the back with Nyx and Persephone, who also needed rides. They'd both come with Hades, but he was returning to the Underworld that night instead of to MOA.

Artemis waved bye to the goddessgirls from the doorway of the temple as the silver reindeer pulling their chariot lifted off. She was staying behind for a bit to thank a group of nymphs and some mortal helpers who had arrived to clean up after the party.

"How's Artemis getting back?" Eos asked, a little

worried that she might be taking that goddessgirl's place in the chariot.

As if reading Eos's thoughts, Athena replied, "The band is sticking around to jam a little. They'll have room for her in their chariot when she's ready to leave."

"Pink!" Eos replied. When all but Nyx quirked their eyebrows at her, she quickly explained that "pink" was her word for "cool."

"I like it!" Aphrodite exclaimed. "Pink *is* cool. It's my favorite color!"

"No, really?" teased Persephone. Which made everyone laugh, including Aphrodite.

As the reindeer zoomed toward MOA, Eos put aside her worries about running into Zeus. She'd overheard several people at Nyx's party say that he was a very busy guy. So it wasn't likely he'd be dropping by the student dorms, even if he'd returned from his tournament by the time the students got back. She'd only be at MOA for the night, gone again before dawn. Odds were extremely low that she'd cross paths with that . . . that . . . *imprisonator*!

Excited about the upcoming sleepover, she turned toward Persephone and Nyx, and the three of them began to chat about this and that. When some godboys flew by on winged sandals, making funny muscle poses and showing off for them, Eos and the other four girls laughed. They flexed their arm muscles doing girl power poses in return.

"Do you hear music?" Eos asked the others a while later. With her hands cupped around her ears, she strained to hear the thin melody that floated in the air.

"It's coming from the Heavens Above chariot," Nyx said, pointing some distance behind them.

Though the band's purple chariot was barely a speck in the sky, it had to be moving at a good clip, since Artemis and the band members had left later than everyone else.

After listening closely for a few moments, Athena said, "I can hear a lyre."

"Apollo, then," Persephone said. "That boy *lives* to play music!"

Reminded of him, Eos promised herself again that somehow, before she went to sleep that night, she'd seek out Apollo. And she'd ask for a prophecy to determine whether she'd be able to make Tithonus immortal. There had to be a way!

6

MOA!

IT WASN'T LONG BEFORE THE SILVER CHARIOT landed at MOA. Eos shouldered her backpack as she, Nyx, Persephone, Athena, and Aphrodite scrambled down from their seats.

"I'll tend to the reindeer," Athena offered. "The rest of you can go on ahead."

"Okay, thanks. See you in a bit," said Aphrodite.

Eos glanced up at the awesome five-story Academy

as she, Nyx, Persephone, and Aphrodite crossed the marble courtyard. She'd never seen the building up close before. She observed its polished white stone walls. Like Artemis's temple, these were surrounded on all sides by dozens of Ionic columns. Sculpted below the building's peaked rooftop she could just make out some low-relief friezes.

The three girls climbed the granite steps to the Academy's entrance. They passed through heavy bronze doors and then continued through a spectacular dome-ceilinged entryway to a marble staircase that led to the upper floors of the Academy.

"Girls' dorm is on the fourth floor, boys' dorm on the fifth," Aphrodite informed Eos as the four girls began to climb the stairs. "You can take my room tonight, since I won't be staying here. I don't have a roommate, so you'll have it all to yourself."

"Aphrodite and I made plans earlier this week to sleep at my house," Persephone explained. "Most of the time I live off campus with my mom."

"That's super nice of you, Aphrodite," said Eos. "Thanks." But then, feeling a little disappointed that the two girls wouldn't be staying, especially since Nyx would have to go soon too, she added, "Does that mean you'll be leaving right away?"

Persephone seemed to sense her disappointment. "Not for a while. We want to have dinner with you and Nyx first."

"And we'll make some time to hang out afterward, too, after Nyx leaves," Aphrodite added as they arrived at the fourth-floor landing. After pushing through the door into the girls' dorm, they started down the hallway, which was lined with doors. "Here we are. My room," Aphrodite announced moments later. She flung open a door on the left.

Immediately, an adorable black-and-white kitten darted out into the hall. "Hey, little fur ball. Not trying to escape, are you?" Persephone cooed as she swept the kitten up in her arms. It gave her cheek a lick with its small pink tongue and she giggled.

Aphrodite smiled at Eos. "That's Adonis. Persephone and I share him. We're taking him with us to her house tonight."

"Hello, sweetie," Eos said to the kitten. She ran a hand over the soft fur along its back. She'd never had a pet. Mostly because she and her mom weren't home a lot. It wouldn't be fair to a cat or dog to be left alone so much of the time. Luckily, she could always pet Tithonus's cat whenever she was at his house.

Eos's eyes widened as the girls entered Aphrodite's

room, which had two beds, two closets, and two built-in desks. "I love how you've decorated!" she enthused. Aphrodite had painted pink and red hearts all over the walls of her room and covered both beds with red velvet comforters stitched with a pattern of little white hearts. Although only one of the beds had a sparkly red fabric canopy draped over it, each had exactly six puffy, heart-shaped pillows neatly arranged at the heads of the beds.

"Thanks," said Aphrodite, sounding pleased.

Guessing that Aphrodite probably slept in the canopied bed, Eos shrugged off her backpack and placed it carefully at the foot of the other bed. Then she and Nyx sat down next to each other on that bed. Meanwhile, Persephone took a seat on Aphrodite's bed, lowered Adonis to her lap, and went on cooing over him while she stroked his soft fur.

Aphrodite opened a tidy-looking closet on the other side of the room. "Since you planned to go home after the party, I'm guessing you didn't pack any overnight things," she said over her shoulder to Eos.

"No, I didn't," Eos confirmed. "But I can just sleep in the clothes I'm wearing."

A horrified look flashed over Aphrodite's face. "No way am I letting you do that! Wear one of my nightgowns," she suggested. She pointed to a large section of them that hung neatly from the bar at the top of her closet.

Eos stepped over to take a look. Pink vapor swirled from her fingers as she riffled through the nightgowns. "Wow! They're all gorgeous. You're so nice to let me borrow one." She finally chose a simple sleeveless rose-colored one with a bit of lace around its neck and hem.

Aphrodite nodded her approval as Eos slipped the nightgown from its hanger. "Good choice," she said.

As Eos laid the nightgown out at the end of her bed, Athena poked her head into the room. "Ready to go have dinner?" she asked them.

Persephone looked up from petting Adonis. "Sure! I ate a lot of snacks at the temple, but my stomach's on empty again."

"So's mine," said Aphrodite, as Eos nodded in agreement.

"Mine, too," said Nyx. She glanced out the window at the far side of the room. "I should have just enough time to eat before I need to go do my job."

On the way to the cafeteria, Eos got a chance to marvel at the Academy's many statues, golden fountains, and gleaming marble floors. She stood for a few moments to study the domed ceiling she'd only just glimpsed on the way in. It was covered with paintings illustrating the glorious exploits of the gods and goddesses.

"Impressive, isn't it?" Nyx murmured in her ear.

"That's for sure," Eos replied. She shuddered at the painting of Zeus in battle, though. Driving a chariot pulled by four white horses, he was hurling thunderbolts through the clouds. It could've been any battle, but what if it was the Titanomachy—the war between the Olympians and the Titans? Zeus might have been aiming for her dad, for all she knew!

The roar of many voices and the clinking of plates and utensils greeted Eos's ears as the girls entered the crowded school cafeteria. She glanced around and was pleased to note again that she didn't stand out in the least here. Several students at MOA had wings, for example. She also spotted a boy with a lizard tail and one with the body of a horse—a centaur.

She chuckled at a couple of signs on the cafeteria walls. Signs you'd never see back home at Oceanus Middle School. One read: NO SHAPE-SHIFTING OR FLYING INSIDE THE SCHOOL. The other read: RESPECT PERSONAL SPACE. TAILS AND WINGS CAN BE DANGEROUS THINGS. IF YOU SEE SOMETHING, SAY SOMETHING.

"Hey, there's Artemis!" Nyx called out, pointing toward one of the tables. Artemis spotted the others at almost the exact same moment. She half-stood from her seat and waved to them.

As Eos followed the other girls across the cafeteria floor, pink mist again drifted from her fingertips to float in the air behind her. Nyx had once told her that when she'd first come to MOA to visit, the black mist that sometimes swirled around her (only if she was anxious or startled) had alarmed some students. For whatever reason, a lot of immortals as well as humans were leery of darkness, however. No one at Artemis's temple, and no one here in the cafeteria, either, paid any attention to the pink mist trailing Eos.

Unlike at her own school, here Eos was *normal*. It was nice. Not that she'd ever want to attend MOA, mind you. She could never leave Tithonus or her mom behind. And despite feeling like an outsider at times, she'd carved out a place for herself at her school.

The girls got plates of food and cartons of nectar (from an eight-handed cafeteria lady, no less!), then went to sit with Artemis. "So what is the school you go to like?" Athena asked Eos after everyone was seated.

"Oceanus Middle School is pretty ordinary compared to here, but I like it mostly," Eos answered before digging into her plate of nectaroni. *Mmm.* Noodles made with nectar were simply nectalicious! She didn't tell Athena that she was the only immortal at her school. She didn't want anyone feeling sorry for her. Instead she told them about the track team, and the clubs she had started, and about her best friend, Tithonus, and how he was an expert on bugs.

When Eos talked about Tithonus, Aphrodite's eyes lit up with interest. "You say this boy is your 'best friend,'" she said. But from the way you talk about him, I'm wondering if he's really an *extra-special* friend."

"Well, I *do* think he's extra special," Eos replied. "I guess that's why he's my best friend."

At this the other five girls erupted in giggles.

After a moment of confusion, Eos blushed. "Oh! I get what you're asking now. And, uh, no. We are *not* crushing," she told Aphrodite firmly.

"Yet," the goddessgirl of love and beauty added with a smile.

Eos and Nyx exchanged a grin. Nyx had told her once that Aphrodite saw signs of love everywhere. Eos didn't really care if Aphrodite or any of the other girls (wrongly) suspected her friendship with Tithonus would turn into a crush kind of thing. Still, she was a little relieved when Aphrodite, Athena, and Persephone started to talk about their *actual* crushes instead.

Neither Nyx nor Artemis was paying much attention to the crush talk, Eos noticed. Nyx had begun a side conversation with a girl at the table next to theirs, while Artemis had started sneaking bits of dinner from her plate down to her dogs under the table. However, even Artemis couldn't help laughing with the others now and then as they teased each other about their "extra-special" friends.

Eos polished off her nectaroni, then opened her carton of nectar and took a long sip. "I am sooo thirsty. This tastes good." She and her mom drank nectar every day at home. Gods and goddesses couldn't stay immortal without it!

"Yes, doesn't it?" said Athena. "The fountains here at MOA spout nectar too. I remember how surprised I was by that my first day at the Academy. Mainly at the way it made my skin shimmer."

"Yeah, thank godness for ambrosia and nectar,"

Aphrodite said, fluffing her golden hair with one hand. Her skin, and that of Eos and the other four immortal girls at their table, shimmered a little more brightly since they'd begun sipping the nectar. They looked as if they'd been dusted with a fine golden glitter.

"Hey," Eos began casually. "Is there any way—" Just as she was starting to ask if there was any way nectar could work to change a mortal—Tithonus, to be exact—into an immortal, her hopes were shattered by a green-skinned, snaky-haired girl passing by their table.

"Too bad nectar doesn't work on mortals," the girl announced, having obviously overheard Aphrodite. "Otherwise I'd have shimmery skin and be Medusa the goddessgirl instead of plain ol' Medusa the mortal." She sounded a little grumpy about that.

"True," Persephone commented to Eos as Medusa sailed on past. "Ambrosia and nectar have no effect on mortals."

So that was that, thought Eos. But she wasn't giving up yet. "Is there maybe some spell that could turn them immortal, though?" She eyed the others, hoping this possibility she'd been counting on wouldn't also be crushed.

Nyx raised an eyebrow. Eos wondered if she'd guessed why Eos was asking. But if so, she kept that knowledge to herself. Which was sweet of her.

Athena munched a bit of ambrosia salad thoughtfully, then said, "Technically, yes. But around here only my dad has the power to cast spells to grant immortality to mortals. He did it once, for one day only, for Medusa. As a reward."

Eos's heart sank. Only *Zeus*? Even if she *could* put

aside her anger at him long enough to go ask that he make Tithonus immortal, why would he help her? After all, her dad had fought against him in the war. What if he got mad at her for even daring to ask? She'd heard that sparks flew from his fingers whenever he became excitable. Sparks that could shock a person or singe furniture. Eos had no desire to experience those shocks firsthand, thank you very much. If only she could figure out in advance if Zeus would help her!

As she was pondering all this, Apollo, who'd been sitting with members of his band and some other godboys, came over to the girls' table. "Hey, sis," he said to Artemis. "I'm done eating. Want me to take your dogs for a walk?"

"Yeah," Artemis replied. "That would be great. Then I could finally eat without them snitching food."

Huh? thought Eos. Maybe the dogs had been begging, but Artemis hadn't seemed to mind. She had readily fed them tidbits as the others talked around her. Eos decided Artemis must have been joking. Or at least half-joking.

Apollo whistled to the dogs, and they scrambled from under the table to join him. As he started across the cafeteria with them, Eos panicked. Apollo was her last hope. She couldn't let him leave without talking to him! She guzzled the remainder of her nectar and then abruptly stood. Holding up her empty carton, she said, "Be right back. I need more nectar."

Instead of fetching another carton, though, she hurried to catch up with Apollo. Before he could reach the door, she kneeled to pet Amby, so that he would have to stop. Immediately the beagle lay down on the floor and rolled over onto its back.

"Hey, um, there's something I've been wanting to ask you," she began, looking up at the godboy as she stroked Amby's belly.

Apollo raised his eyebrows. "Yeah? What's that?"

Quickly, Eos explained how she wanted to ask Zeus to help her make a mortal friend of hers immortal.

Apollo's eyes went wide in surprise. "That's a big ask. And probably not something Zeus would agree to, at least not without a very good reason." He paused, and then corrected himself. "Make that a *mega-dozen* good reasons."

"Uh-huh," she said earnestly. "So that's where you come in."

"Me?" His eyes widened even farther.

She paused to gather her argument before speaking. She needed to hurry, though. From the corner of her eye, she could see that Nyx and the other girls at their table had finished eating. They were stacking all the trays to take to the tray return and were beginning to stand up. Soon they'd be heading toward her and Apollo.

Eos jumped up from her crouch. "I . . . um . . . I was wondering—hoping, really—if you could summon a prophecy to reveal whether or not Zeus will grant my request. Before I bother to ask him and risk incurring his thunderbolty wrath."

"I can answer that one, easy-peasy," Apollo said at once. "Because I don't need to foresee anything to predict that he won't grant it."

"But couldn't you maybe do an official prophecy for me?" Eos begged. "I'll dedicate a dawn to you," she offered. "I know it's not much, but it's all I—"

"Not necessary, but thanks," Apollo told her.

Beyond him, Nyx and the other goddessgirls were now moving toward the tray return. And Artemis's three dogs were getting a little antsy, pacing around her and Apollo's feet. After a few moments' hesitation, he finally let out a long sigh. "I can see this is very important to you, so I'll try."

"Thanks," Eos said eagerly.

"Don't thank me yet," Apollo cautioned her. "You probably won't like what I'm able to see."

Before she could assure him she'd be grateful for whatever he could tell her, Apollo squeezed his eyes shut. His face went expressionless. After a few seconds of silence, his eyes popped open. With a surprised look on his face he told her, "It seems that Zeus will grant your request!"

"He will?" Joy flooded over Eos, and she did a little happy dance right then and there that set the dogs to bouncing excitedly with her. "This is the best news ever! I—and, uh, my friend—can't thank you enough!"

"No problem," said Apollo. The dogs had begun to paw at his legs in their eagerness to get going. "Good luck!" he told her as he started toward the door again. But after just a couple of steps, he turned back. Cocking his head at her, he said, "I'm curious about something, though."

"What's that?" Eos asked distractedly. The other goddessgirls had dropped off their trays and were coming toward her.

Apollo gave her a long look. "Are you sure your friend *wants* to be immortal?"

The question startled Eos. "Sure, why wouldn't he? Medusa does," she blurted. She'd never actually asked Tithonus, but it seemed like a no-brainer that he'd want to be a godboy. After all, if he became one, in addition to them getting to be friends forever, he'd have all the time in the world to study his precious bugs!

Apollo shrugged. "You're probably right. I just thought it was a question worth asking." He hesitated before adding, "Please don't tell any other students around here about my prophecy. I don't want them all coming to me for prophecies of their own."

"I won't tell, promise," Eos said hurriedly as the other goddessgirls came toward her. "Thanks, Apollo. I really appreciate it."

"Sure. Later," he said. Then he headed off, whistling for the dogs to follow him from the cafeteria.

7

Zeus

WHAT WERE YOU TALKING TO MY BROTHER about?" Artemis asked Eos as the two of them and Nyx exited the cafeteria behind Persephone, Aphrodite, and Athena.

"Not much," Eos replied vaguely, wanting to keep her promise to Apollo. "I was just petting your dogs and stuff." Luckily, Artemis seemed satisfied with this answer and didn't press her further. Nyx didn't either. *Phew!*

Since it was close to seven by now, the girls all said good-bye to Nyx when they reached the base of the marble staircase that led up to classrooms and dorms. Eos was last to give her a hug. "Thanks for inviting me to your celebration," she said. "It was a lot of fun."

"I'm glad you were able to come," Nyx replied. "Enjoy yourself tonight, and I'll see you at dawn." Then she waved to the girls and quickly disappeared through the Academy's front doors.

"So . . . um . . . do you think your dad might be back from that tournament he went to?" Eos asked Athena as the girls started upstairs. Now that she knew for sure that Zeus would grant her request to make Tithonus immortal, she was eager to see him.

Athena nodded. "He flew in on his winged horse, Pegasus, while I was giving the reindeer their food and water. He's probably in his office, since he told me he had some work he needed to do tonight." With one foot on the bottom step of the stairs, she paused. Raising her eyebrows at Eos, she added, "Sounds to me like there *is* something you want to see him about, after all."

"Yes, actually, there is," Eos said, reversing the emphatic no she'd given on their chariot trip back from Ephesus.

The other three girls had bunched around them on the stairs and looked at her expectantly. It was obvious they were curious to know her business with Zeus.

"I . . . um . . ." Suddenly Eos remembered Tithonus's request before she left for the unveiling.

"I want to ask for his autograph for a friend of mine!" she blurted out. "He asked me to try to get it if I saw Zeus."

Aphrodite grinned. "Would this be your *extra-special* friend we're talking about?"

Eos felt her cheeks flush. "Well, yeah."

"Piece of cake," said Athena. "Zeus loves signing autographs for mortal fans."

"Want someone to go with you?" Persephone asked. "The rest of us can start organizing some games upstairs in the dorm. We were thinking that would be a fun way for you to get to know some of the other girls before Aphrodite and I leave for my mom's."

"Thanks, but I'd kind of like to meet Zeus on my own," Eos replied. Truthfully, she wasn't looking forward to meeting him at all, but for Tithonus's sake she would. And she would have loved the girls' company for moral support. But just as Apollo didn't want word getting around that he'd given her a prophecy lest other students start asking for them too, she guessed Zeus wouldn't want it known that he'd granted her friend immortality. If that news got out, he'd no doubt have a stream of mortals like Medusa coming to him with the same request!

After saying good-bye to the other four goddess-girls, Eos followed signs to the main office. There she met a nine-headed lady, whose name tag read MS. HYDRA.

"Is Principal Zeus in?" Eos asked her.

Ms. Hydra had been filing papers behind a tall counter, but now all nine of her heads swiveled toward Eos. "And who might you be?" demanded a grumpy-looking green head.

"Eos. Goddessgirl of the dawn," she replied. "I was hoping to see Zeus tonight since I have to leave MOA super early tomorrow to do my job."

Ms. Hydra's heads arched their eyebrows. "Did Principal Zeus give permission for you to stay the night?" her gray head asked briskly.

"Well, no," Eos admitted. "But Hera did. We were both at the unveiling of Nyx's statue at Artemis's temple in Ephesus, and—" Hearing thumps and grunts coming from behind a door at the far side of the main office, she broke off speaking and looked toward the sound.

"Principal Zeus is very busy at present," the office lady's purple head said with an impatient sniff. "It's after hours and we'll both be leaving soon. You'll have to come back tomorrow."

"Puh-leeze? I won't be here tomorrow. Like I said,

I have to leave super early because of my job." As soon as the words were out of her mouth it occurred to her that, since bringing the dawn only took a half hour or so to complete, she *could* return to MOA to speak to Zeus afterward. But she wanted to get this over with before she lost her nerve. So she smiled her most winning smile and coaxed, "It won't take long. I just need to ask him a question."

While more thumps and grunts came from beyond the door across the way, Ms. Hydra's heads argued among themselves about whether or not to grant Eos's request. Finally the office lady's sunny-looking yellow head extended its neck toward Eos and said, "I'll see if he's willing to be disturbed." Ms. Hydra came out from behind the tall counter and crossed the room to knock on Principal Zeus's office door.

"Enter!" thundered Zeus.

Eos cringed at his loud voice, and a shiver ran down her spine. Maybe this wasn't such a good idea after all. If not for Apollo's prophecy assuring her that Zeus would grant her request, she might have chickened out then and there. Instead, as Ms. Hydra opened Zeus's door and then stuck two of her heads inside the room, Eos tried to peek in around her. But the partly open door blocked her view.

"Visiting student here to see you," Eos heard one of Ms. Hydra's heads announce to Zeus. "Name is Eos, goddessgirl of the dawn." Then another head, probably the impatient purple one, said, "I told her you're busy and it's late, so if you'd rather not see her . . ."

"Not a problem. Show her in!" Zeus's booming voice replied. "Four hundred forty, four hundred forty-one . . ."

Huh? What was he doing in there? Eos wondered. Counting an enormous pile of bronze and silver drachmas?

Ms. Hydra withdrew her two heads. Then all nine of them nodded at Eos. "Go on in," they chorused before heading back to the front desk.

Eos tried without success to calm the butterflies in her stomach as she stepped inside Zeus's office. Her eyes went to his enormous desk. The large golden throne behind it had fancy back and seat cushions in blue and gold, MOA school colors. And it was empty.

"Welcome to MOA," a loud voice boomed at her. She swung around, her gaze shooting deeper into the room to find the red-haired, red-bearded Zeus lying on his back on the floor. His two muscular arms were lifting a four-drawer file cabinet high above his chest. "Four hundred fifty-seven, four hundred fifty-eight . . . ," he huffed as he pumped it up and down, grunting with the effort.

"Hera told me she'd invited you here. Forgot to tell Ms. Hydra, though." Then he went on counting and grunting, without looking at her.

"That's okay," said Eos. That file cabinet looked mega-heavy. Zeus started pumping it with only one hand, then tossing it back and forth between his left and his right! She stepped back, wary of such strength.

"So what do you need?" he asked. "Did it just *dawn* on you that since you were here you should take the opportunity to meet the King of the Gods and Ruler of the Heavens?" he added with a big laugh. "Four hundred ninety, four hundred ninety-one . . ."

Zeus made jokes? This was unexpected. "Um.

Not exactly, but . . . ," Eos began, nervously shifting from one foot to the other.

"You're Helios's little sister, right?" Zeus roared out as she debated how best to word her request. "Great guy, Helios. *Sunny* personality. Ha-ha!"

"Uh . . . yeah," Eos murmured. Definitely a joke. Weird. She wasn't sure what she'd expected Zeus to be like or how she'd thought he'd treat her, but certainly not like this. He was being so . . . so *nice*. It actually kind of rattled her.

"Go on. . . . Four hundred ninety-seven . . . Four hundred ninety-eight . . . So why did you really come to see me?" he boomed.

"Five hundred!" he exclaimed after two more pushes. "Done!" Zeus tossed the file cabinet onto the bottoms of his huge sandaled feet. Still lying on his back, he pumped his legs in the air, twirling the file cabinet around and around like some circus performer. Too nervous to speak now, Eos took another couple of steps back and glanced toward the open office door.

When she said nothing more, Zeus regarded her with his intense blue eyes. "Well?" he thundered. "Speak up. What are you here for?"

Eos gulped. After clearing her throat, she drew on all her courage and said, "I have this friend back home. His name is Tithonus? He's mortal, and I was wondering if—"

"Stop right there!" ordered Zeus. He kicked the cabinet from his feet, causing it to land a few yards away from him, standing upright on the floor. *Bam!* With that he leaped up and strode over to loom above her. All seven feet of him. Sparks of electricity zinged and popped from his arms and fingers as he planted his hands on his hips.

Eos gulped again. Her eyes slid sideways, taking in all the scorch marks on the office walls. Then her eyes found the door again. "Uh . . . maybe I should just go. . . ."

Suddenly Zeus took hold of her arm. *Bzzt!* "Ow! Wait!" she said, feeling a few sparks lightly zap her. He didn't let go, but instead steered her to one of the visitor chairs set in a row before his desk. As she stood, somewhat dazed, next to the chair, Zeus plopped down on the golden throne opposite.

"Sit!" he commanded, and she did. Her chair's cushion was covered with small scorch marks too, she noticed with alarm.

Electricity fizzled from Zeus's fingers as he steepled them together on top of his desk. He leaned forward, his muscular arms bulging. "I think I know what you're about to ask," he told her.

Eos jumped in her chair. "You d-do?" she stuttered.

Zeus rolled his eyes. Then he kicked back in his chair and crossed his sandaled feet on his desktop. A stack of papers on it fluttered haphazardly to the floor, but he took no notice. "You want me to make your friend immortal, right?"

Eos blinked in surprise. Had he somehow read her mind?

Zeus sighed. "If I had a drachma for every time someone asked that favor of me, I'd be even richer than I already am."

Eos's heart fell. "So you won't do it? But Apollo prophesied that you *would*!" She hadn't meant to tell Zeus about the prophecy, but Apollo had only asked her not to tell any *students*, so she really hadn't broken her promise.

Zeus's bushy red eyebrows shot up. "A *prophecy?* Well, that changes things!" Getting up from his desk, he began to pace around the room, muttering to himself. Though Eos strained to hear, she couldn't make out even a single word. At last Zeus stopped in front of her. "Can you remember exactly what you asked and what Apollo said?" he asked gruffly.

Eos nodded. His prophecy was etched on her brain! "First I asked Apollo if you would help me make Tithonus immortal," she told Zeus. "And then he said: 'It seems that Zeus will grant your request.'"

"I see," said Zeus. He folded both arms over his chest and looked at her with a thoughtful expression on his face. "The thing is, immortality can be a tricky gift to grant. You say you asked Apollo if I would help *you* make your friend immortal. So because of the way you phrased your question, I'll have to lend you some of my power instead of doing the job myself. I have no choice. Prophecies must be obeyed." He set a hand on her shoulder. "I hereby give you the power to grant your friend immortality when you see him next." A strange tingling zapped through her and then was gone.

It was a moment before the realization of what he'd done dawned on the goddessgirl of the dawn. "Wait! I really wanted *you* to make Tithonus immortal! What if I don't do it right—"

"Too late," interrupted Zeus. "What's done is done." He strode to his office door. "Now I'm off. Got a chess match to win! Against your dad!"

"Huh?" Her *dad*? Eos stared at him, astonished at how casually Zeus had mentioned him.

"You mean down in the Underworld? Where you imprisoned him?" She didn't tell him she had never visited her dad there even once.

Hearing the tension in her voice, Zeus nodded sympathetically. "I know his imprisonment must not seem fair to you, but war is like chess. Two sides. Winners, losers. Your dad's not a bad fellow. It's just that he wound up on the wrong side in this war, and . . . well . . . rules are rules. Losers in war must go to Tartarus in the Underworld."

"You're right—it doesn't seem fair!" she insisted.

"I can understand how you feel," Zeus said in a surprisingly gentle voice. "But I made the rules of war long ago to cut down on strife in the world. Your dad's comfortable down there, though—lots of hobbies and studies. And he's become a first-class chess master. I've been practicing at tournaments in hopes I can finally beat him one day."

Her dad was *comfortable* in the depths of the

Underworld? He played *chess*? This was not at all what she had imagined his life there to be like. With the exception of Nyx's home, Hades' famous palace, and the Elysian Fields (the Underworld's most desirable neighborhood, where everyone feasted, played, and sang for forevermore), she'd thought the Underworld was all doom and gloom!

A competitive gleam lit Zeus's eyes. "And I have a feeling that tonight's the night I'm finally going to win!" Looking determined, he stomped off toward the door.

Eos turned in her chair, so she could watch him over her shoulder. Pausing in the doorway, he informed her, "Remember, this whole immortality-granting power I gave you is just a one-time thing. Also, your borrowed power will expire twenty-four hours from now."

Yikes! thought Eos. That meant she only had until tomorrow evening to make Tithonus immortal! Stunned at all Zeus had just told her, she sat glued to her chair for several moments.

But at last she jumped up. "Wait! How do I do it? What are the words to use?" She dashed through the door, past Ms. Hydra, and out into the hall.

Zeus, however, was gone.

Eos stood there uncertainly. Was there a special spell she should use, or what? she wondered. Confusion swirled in her brain. Not just about the spell, either. There was the dad stuff too. What was she supposed to make of all that Zeus had told her?

8

A Blight Misunderstanding

EOS WAS STILL STANDING IN THE HALL OUTSIDE

the main office when Ares bounded up to her. "Thank godness, I found you!" he exclaimed breath- lessly. "Apollo told me you'd gone to see Zeus, but I wasn't sure you'd still be around. C'mon, I need your help!"

He grabbed her hand. His blue eyes were big and round. He looked almost . . . scared. *Scared?* The godboy of war? No way! The very idea momentarily put thoughts of immortality spells and her dad right out of her head.

"What's wrong?" she asked Ares as he began tugging her down the hall.

He looked over his shoulder at her, but didn't stop moving. "Back at Artemis's temple, when you asked me for my autograph, you mentioned that your friend . . . um . . . *Titmouse*?"

"Tithonus," Eos corrected.

Ares nodded, which caused a lock of his blond hair to fall forward over one eye, just like Tithonus's cowlick often did. "Yeah, *him*," Ares said, shoving back the unruly lock. A while ago he'd been voted handsomest godboy in a *Teen Scrollazine* reader poll. Eos supposed he was, but only if you were into annoying, blond-haired, super-athletic boys.

If she ever *were* to have a crush, she'd choose someone gentler and more modest than the godboy of war. Someone with a grand passion for things and a sense of humor, too. Someone more like . . . well . . . *Tithonus*. Not that she'd ever admit that to anyone. Especially not Aphrodite, who saw romance blooming everywhere she looked!

"Wait. Stop. Where are we going?" asked Eos. She tugged on his hand and Ares paused, letting go of her.

"You said your friend was a bug expert, and you sometimes help him." Ares rubbed the back of his neck, looking uncomfortable. "So you know about bugs. And, uh, I was wondering if you could, uh, *identify* a spider I found in my room. I'm worried it could be poisonous."

"Well," said Eos, "I've picked up a few things from

Tithonus, but he's the true expert. And spiders aren't actually bugs. Or insects, for that matter. They're *arachnids*. They have eight legs, instead of six, no wings or antennae, either. Plus, they can't chew."

"See?" Ares flashed her a blinding white smile. "You do know a lot about . . . er . . . *arachnids*." Suddenly he paled, and his anxiety seemed to return. "Won't you please at least come take a look at my, er, problem?" Seeming to assume she wouldn't tell him no, he took her hand again, tugging her toward the end of the hall.

Eos followed, suspicious now. Was it possible this big, athletic godboy of war was *afraid* of spiders? Yes, it was. Lots of people were. She wasn't that crazy about them herself. But being around Tithonus had made her much less afraid of arachnids—and insects as well—than she might've been otherwise.

Deciding she owed Ares a favor since he'd been so nice about signing his autograph for Tithonus, she said, "Okay. I'll take a look. But I'm not promising I can identify it."

"Great!" Ares said. "Follow me!" Letting go of her hand, he took off up the wide marble staircase so fast that she had to practically run to keep pace with him.

As they hurried up to the dorms, Eos tried to calm him down. The more he learned about spiders, the less afraid he might become. "So my friend Tithonus told me spiders aren't actually poisonous. But some are *venomous*. Which means they inject their toxins with fangs." She was surprised she'd remembered that. Maybe her attention was less scattered than she gave herself credit for!

Remembering something else, she added, "And

though almost all spiders have venom, which they use to weaken their prey, the venom seldom has any effect on humans. Bees and wasps are far more dangerous. In fact, only a tiny fraction of one percent of spider species in the entire world have venom strong enough to make people sick."

They'd reached the third-floor landing by now, and she paused for a second to catch her breath. "So the spider in your room is probably completely harmless," she concluded.

"Too much information. No more, please," Ares begged in a shaky voice. So much for calming him down.

As they blew past the fourth-floor landing and started up to the boys' dorm on the fifth floor, Eos heard the door to the girls' dorm open. Shouts and laughter streamed out through it. The games

145

Persephone and the other girls had been organizing must already be in progress, Eos realized with longing.

She glanced back to see who had just come out. It was a girl with short orange hair and cute iridescent orange wings. *Pheme*, the goddessgirl of gossip. For a second their eyes met.

"Come on, Eos! We're almost there!" Ares called from a few steps above her. Hearing his voice, Pheme's eyes rounded in surprise. Without a word to Eos, she turned around and hurried back inside the girls' dorm.

Weird, thought Eos. But then she figured that Pheme had probably just forgotten something she needed and gone back inside to get whatever it was.

When they reached the fifth-floor landing, Ares came to a halt before the hall door. "Normally girls aren't allowed in the boys' dorm and vice versa," he told Eos. "But this is an emergency!"

"We don't have to break the rule," Eos told him. "You could just capture the spider and bring it—" She stopped speaking when she noticed that Ares had gone quite pale. Wow! He really *must* be afraid of spiders. If he weren't an immortal, she'd even say he was *deathly* afraid of them! "Okay, I'll go with you," she said.

He gave her another shaky smile. "Thanks." Then he opened the door. "Girl in the hall!" he yelled out to warn any guys who might be about.

"*Eek!*" a boy's voice squealed. Peering around Ares, Eos glimpsed Poseidon. Wrapped in a dolphin-patterned towel and with a puffy sea-blue shower cap over his head, he scurried down the hall into what was probably the bathroom.

Stifling a giggle, Eos followed Ares to his room. It was fascinating to be in such unfamiliar territory, and her eyes darted here and there, taking it all in. The messy hallway was littered with archery bows, swords, and clubs, and also what appeared to be school projects in progress, such as a half-built model of an amphitheater and one of an arena.

She almost tripped over someone's stray sandal when she noticed a life-size suit of armor farther down the hall. The armored "knight" held a shield in one hand and a spear in the other. "That armor is too cool for school!" she exclaimed.

Ares turned to look at her. "Thanks. My sister and I built it when we were kids. I put a spell on it so it could talk."

"No joke. Really?" said Eos as they came even with the "knight." All at once it came to life, raising its spear and pointing it at her chest. "Halt. Who goes there?" it demanded to know.

Eos sucked in her breath.

"Relax," Ares told the armor. "She's my guest."

At this the "knight" lowered its spear. *Creak!* It bowed at the waist. "Pardon me, m'lady," it said to Eos. "'Twas a grievous mistake. To be certain, I meant thee no harm."

"None taken," Eos assured it. For some reason she found herself curtsying.

"Here's my room," Ares told her. He opened a door just beyond the suit of armor. Standing back, he gestured politely for Eos to enter first. At least she *thought* he was being polite. Then again, maybe he only wanted her to go first because he feared the spider might be lying in wait for him or something!

Eos stepped inside and glanced around. Like

Aphrodite's room (and probably most of the rooms in both the girls' and boys' dorms), this one had two matching beds, two closets, two desks, and one window, which stood open. But there the similarity ended, because Ares' room was nowhere near as tidy as Aphrodite's.

And the style of decoration here could best be described as "athletic." Various weapons and shields, as well as posters with war scenes or battle maps, adorned the walls. Barbells and weights sat atop one desk. There was a set of half-painted gladiator army men and a paint set on the opposite desk. Both blankets on the beds were boring brown.

"*Psst.* It was on the wall above my desk—the one with the army—when I saw it last," Ares said in a loud whisper. He was still in the hall, eyeing the area around his desk from the doorway. Why the whisper? Did he think the spider might hear him and attack? He still hadn't ventured inside, so perhaps fear really *had* driven his "politeness."

Eos went over to his desk and thoroughly searched on top of it and the surrounding wall. "Well, the spider's not here anymore," she reported. She studied the ceiling, deciding to widen the search. The spider would likely be easy to spot if it was still in Ares' room. It had to be *huge* to have frightened him so much.

Suddenly Ares let out a shriek from the doorway. "Aaagh! There it is!"

Eos wheeled toward him as he pointed to the floor near one of the closets. At first all she saw was a balled-up dirty sock. But then she saw movement near the sock. An itsy-bitsy spider, no bigger than her smallest toenail, scurried across the floor in

Ares' direction. She stifled the urge to laugh when the godboy of war leaped away, moving backward into the hall.

"What's going on?" asked a voice. A couple of godboys had rushed over behind him and were peering inside the room.

"Nothing. No problem," said Ares, herding them away before they could ask more questions.

Meanwhile, thinking fast, Eos grabbed a crumpled-up piece of papyrus from his trash can. She smoothed it out and then slid it under the spider. Carefully she carried the arachnid to Ares' open window. "Have a nice life, itsy-bitsy spider," she said as she gently transferred it to the wall outside the window.

When she turned around, the other boys were gone and Ares had moved to stand a foot or so inside the room. He jerked his head toward the window, then caught her eye, still looking nervous, though not frantic any longer. "It might crawl back inside."

So Eos closed the window. "Better?" she asked with a smile.

Ares ventured into his room a little farther. "Yeah. Was it a poison—I mean, a *venomous* spider?"

Eos shrugged. "Doubtful. But anyway, it's gone now."

"I owe you," he said.

She smiled. "Consider the debt paid. You gave me your autograph for Tithonus, remember?" But after a moment's thought, she asked, "But actually, there is one thing. Do you have any advice for casting tricky spells?"

Ares lifted an eyebrow. "Define 'tricky spells.'"

"Um . . . like one for granting immortality, for example?"

Ares let out a low whistle. "That *is* a tricky one. So tricky that only Zeus can do it."

"But suppose you *could* cast it. What words would you use?" Eos asked, without revealing that Zeus had lent her his power to do it a single time.

Ares shrugged. "Carefully chosen ones that exactly suit my intentions." After a short pause he added, "And it's always good to use rhyme."

Eos angled her head, a little confused. "That's it?"

"Pretty much," said Ares. Then he waved her back out into the hall. "C'mon, let's get you outta here."

Some of the guys they passed when they left Ares' room looked at her in surprise. She'd broken a rule by being there, she realized. "Hey, she just wanted an autograph for her mortal friend Tithonus," Ares fibbed. "What can I say? I'm popular!"

Eos hoped none of the boys had noticed him signing his autograph for her at Artemis's temple earlier that day. Then again, even if they had, they might think she'd lost it. Or returned for a *second* autograph.

"Hey, uh, don't say anything to anyone about that spider, okay?" Ares whispered to her out of the side of his mouth as they headed up the hall.

"Okay," Eos whispered back. Seeing no one up ahead, she added, "But you shouldn't be embarrassed. Lots of people have phobias about one thing or another. Some people are scared of the dark. Others are scared of—"

Ares straightened his shoulders. "I am the godboy of war. I am *not* scared! Of. Anything!" he insisted. "It's just that my older sister, Eris, used to tease me that there were spiders in my bed when I was little. *Really* little. Like two years old. She said they would spin a web around me while I was sleeping and eat me as a snack." He shuddered.

"Yikes," said Eos. "No wonder you're afraid of them. Well, I promise I won't say a word."

"I told you, I'm not afraid! Now pretty please just be a sweetheart and don't tell—" As he opened the door to the landing, his words broke off.

For there, waiting on the landing with a thunderous scowl on her face, was Aphrodite. "'Sweetheart'? Did I just hear my crush call another girl 'sweetheart'? Another girl who is in the *boys' dorm hall* instead of joining in the games my friends and I planned just for her tonight?" Her voice rose higher and got louder with every word. "Pheme told me I'd find you both here, but I didn't believe it . . . till now." Beneath her anger she looked hurt, thought Eos.

"He didn't mean it the way you're thinking," Eos protested, wanting to calm Aphrodite's fears. Too late she recalled that the goddessgirl of love and beauty, though super nice most of the time, also had a reputation for jealousy. Especially where her crush was concerned. Suddenly Eos could guess why Pheme had rushed back inside the girls' dorm earlier. To tell Aphrodite that she'd seen Eos with Ares!

"Then why are you here exactly?" Aphrodite demanded in a suspicious voice. Hands on hips, the furious goddessgirl glared at Eos. "And don't tell me you came to get Ares' autograph! I saw you ask for it at Artemis's temple. Now I'm thinking that was probably just an excuse to flirt with him."

"What? No!" Eos protested. At the same time, she

remembered Aphrodite frowning at her back at the temple and realized she'd been right about what the goddessgirl had been thinking. That there was flirting going on when there wasn't! Eos looked pleadingly at Ares, willing him to explain about the spider since she couldn't do it herself. Because that would mean breaking a promise!

Ares' mouth flapped open and shut. "I . . . um . . . we . . . er . . . Eos was telling me about bugs!" he blurted at last.

Aphrodite's head jerked back a little. "Bugs?" she echoed in a disbelieving tone.

"That's right," Eos said brightly. "They can be very fascinating."

"Really?" said Aphrodite. It was clear from her tone that she was not buying their story.

Eos just gave her a weak grin and nodded. The other goddessgirl's pretty blue eyes narrowed. A strange light came into them as she folded her arms across her chest. "I guess you must *love* bugs if you find them so fascinating," she said to Eos.

"Well, I wouldn't go *that* far," Eos replied.

Aphrodite's lips curled in irritation.

The sudden sound of footsteps coming up the stairs caused everyone to fall silent. Seconds later, Persephone appeared. "Hey! Pheme told me you all might be up here," she said, looking curiously at Ares and the girls. Then, speaking to Aphrodite, she added, "My mom's here to give us a ride to my house. I already took Adonis to her. You ready to go?"

"Yep," Aphrodite snapped. "I just need to grab my overnight bag from my room."

"Great! I'll let my mom know you'll meet us at her chariot in a few," Persephone said. Then she turned and gave Eos a quick hug. "Great meeting you. Hope I'll see you again sometime."

"Yeah, fun to meet you, too," said Eos.

As Persephone ran back downstairs, Aphrodite glanced over at Eos and Ares. She stared hard at Eos, and a slow, disturbing smile spread over her face. "Well, gotta go. I hope you'll be comfy in my room tonight." She let out a giggle. Then in a singsong voice she added, "Good night. Sleep tight. Don't let the bedbugs bite." This old-fashioned saying, which Eos had only ever heard grown-ups or Tithonus use before, basically meant you hoped the sleeper would get a good night's rest.

"Uh . . . thanks," Eos said in surprise. It seemed that all was forgiven, despite the fact that there was nothing she or Ares needed Aphrodite to forgive them *for*!

"So . . . um . . . I guess I'll see you tomorrow when you get back?" Ares said to Aphrodite.

The beautiful goddessgirl smiled easily at him. "Sure."

Ares gave her a crushy kind of smile in return and sent a casual good-bye wave to Eos before disappearing into the boys' dorm hall again.

Something still felt a little off with Aphrodite, though, thought Eos as they trooped downstairs together. Much to her relief, Artemis and Athena soon joined them. "Too bad you missed the games," Artemis said to Eos.

"Yeah, I know. I'm really sorry I didn't make it," Eos replied earnestly.

"A bunch of us are meeting at the Supernatural

Market to get shakes and snacks now. Want to come?" Athena asked.

Eos peeked over at Aphrodite. Seeing that the girl didn't look mad, she relaxed a little. "Sounds like fun," Eos told Athena and Artemis.

When the girls reached the fourth-floor landing, they paused for a few minutes while Aphrodite ran to her room to grab her overnight bag. Once she was back, they trooped down the rest of the stairs and then pushed out through MOA's main doors. Persephone was holding the black-and-white Adonis in her arms while she and her mom stood waiting at the edge of the torchlit courtyard in a chariot drawn by two magnificent winged serpents.

"Bye, then," Aphrodite said to Eos. They hugged, but it seemed to Eos that Aphrodite's hug was a little stiff. Maybe she only imagined it, though. She hoped so, anyway. She didn't want to part on bad terms.

As Aphrodite started toward the chariot to join Persephone, Artemis and Athena linked arms with Eos, one on either side of her. The three of them began to walk toward the market. "No dogs?" Eos asked Artemis, suddenly noticing the absence of those three bouncy, furry creatures.

"In my room," Artemis replied. "They're not allowed inside the market."

Behind them, Eos didn't notice Aphrodite pause in the middle of the courtyard. And she didn't hear her mutter a spell while staring squarely at Eos's back. If Eos *had* heard the spell, she would have realized that Aphrodite was definitely still jealous:

> *From among the bugs you see,*
> *You will fall in love with three.*

While this spell is in effect,

Other spells will redirect.

These love bugs you must protect!"

When she finished the spell, Aphrodite's pink-glossed lips curved upward with satisfaction, as if she was thinking, *That'll teach her.*

9

Love Bugs

WHEN THEY ARRIVED AT THE SUPERNATURAL Market, Eos, Athena, and Artemis threaded their way through racks of 'zines and shelves of snacks to some round tables at the back of the shop. While Artemis went to get shakes, Eos and Athena joined a group of MOA students that included snaky-haired Medusa; Athena's roommate, Pandora; violet-eyed Dionysus; Eros, the red-cheeked, gold-winged godboy of love; and others.

"You're Eos, right? I'm Amphitrite," said a girl with flowing turquoise hair as Eos sat down across from her.

"Yes, I am. Hi," Eos greeted the girl. Then, suddenly, the name Amphitrite struck a bell and she exclaimed, "I've heard about you! You designed that cool garden at the bottom of the Aegean Sea, right?"

"You know about that?" Amphitrite said in surprise. She was a mermaid, but you'd never guess it, since her tail transformed into legs and feet whenever she was on land.

"My mom's into gardening," Eos explained, leaning closer to be heard over other conversations around them. "She showed me an article about you with a picture of your garden in the *Greekly Weekly News* a while ago. It looked mega-awesome!" That had been one of the rare evenings she and her mom had spent together in the past few months, which was probably why she remembered it.

The turquoise-haired goddessgirl beamed at Eos. "Thanks!"

Just then Artemis returned with a tray of shakes. "Ambrosia? Or nectar?" she asked Eos and the other kids nearby.

"Um . . . can I have one of each?" Eos replied. She could get shakes back home, but none that were ambrosia- or nectar-flavored. This might be her only chance to taste such shakes!

Artemis grinned. "Sure, I got extras of everything." She set two shakes in front of Eos. Amphitrite took a nectar one, then turned to answer a question from Medusa.

"Mmm. This is yummy!" Eos murmured, taking a sip of her ambrosia shake first. She'd only drunk about a quarter of it when Pheme showed up.

"Hi, Eos!" she said brightly. "How's your visit to MOA going?" Her words puffed into the air above her in little cloud letters that swiftly faded away.

Though miffed at the girl for causing trouble by telling Aphrodite she'd seen Eos with Ares, Eos decided not to bring this up. What would be the point? As the goddessgirl of gossip, Pheme had merely acted according to her nature. So, setting aside her annoyance, Eos smiled and gave the orange-haired girl a thumbs-up, replying, "Terrific!" Then she watched as Pheme took a seat beside Eros one table over. From the fond looks the two exchanged, she could guess they were crushing.

Eos spent a pleasant hour or so chatting with Athena and Artemis and the other MOA-ers at their table while sipping her two shakes. (Both were so delish she couldn't decide which flavor she liked best!) But then she began to yawn. "Sorry," she said when Artemis caught her stifling a big one. "I usually go to bed early since I have to get up so early to bring the dawn."

"No apology needed," said Artemis. "I'm kind of tired myself."

"Me too," said Athena. "It's got to be after nine already."

After saying good-bye to the other students, the three girls left the market and started walking back to MOA. Luckily Selene's moon was up in the sky, and it shone super brightly tonight, lighting their path. Along the way, Eos told Athena and Artemis about her urn-room at home. "I get into it by transforming into a mist and whirling down through the opening at the top," she explained. She twirled in circles and transformed briefly to demonstrate this ability of hers.

"That's so . . . *pink*!" Athena exclaimed, copying Eos's word for "cool." "I like to transform into an owl sometimes."

"I changed myself into a stag once," said Artemis as they continued to walk.

What fun this is! Eos thought. Back home, she never got to have conversations about transformation. No one else at her school had any experience with that ability. She was about to ask Artemis why she had changed herself into a male deer when she happened to spy two small, shiny, black beetles under the edge of a nearby bush.

A sudden, strange feeling compelled her to stop. "Wait!" she called to Athena and Artemis. Kneeling, she picked up the two beetles, which were each about a half inch long. Then she stood again and showed them to the other two goddessgirls. "Aren't they the cutest coleoptera you've ever seen?" she enthused, recalling more of what Tithonus had told her over the years.

"Collie-up-to-what?" asked Artemis. "They look like plain old beetles to me."

"They are. All beetles belong to the insect order Coleoptera." With a gentle fingertip, Eos petted first one beetle's and then the other's shiny black elytra, the hardened front pair of wings that protected their fragile hind wings.

"Oh, I get it," said Athena, leaning in to study the insect pair. "The word 'coleoptera' must come from *koleos*, which means 'sheath,' and *ptera*, which means 'wings.'"

"Sure, everybody knows that," Artemis teased her brainy friend.

Athena flicked her a grin. "So as I was saying, Coleoptera must refer to the beetle's sheathlike wings."

Cupping her hands around the two beetles so they wouldn't escape, Eos cooed to them. "Hey, cuties. I'm going to keep you beetely-weetelies as pets!"

Athena grinned as the girls began to walk again. "I think you must have been bitten by the same bug as your friend Tithonus," she told Eos. "You know, as in you're starting to kind of fall in love with insects too!"

Eos parted her hands a crack and smiled dream-ily at the two beetles. "Hmm. My little love bugs." Probably thinking she was joking, the other two girls laughed. But she *wasn't* joking. Which was kind of weird, now that she thought about it. Since when did she love bugs? And why was she nicknaming two beetles "love bugs" when beetles were actually insects, and not especially lovable ones either? What was going on here?

"Personally, I think dogs make better pets," Artemis remarked as the girls kept on walking. "You can't play ball with a beetle."

"Unless it's a dung beetle," said Athena. When the other two looked at her in surprise, she added, "What? It's true. They push around a ball made of dung, also known as poop."

"My beetles aren't that kind, but they'll be easier to take care of than dogs," Eos commented as the girls crossed MOA's marble courtyard. "For one thing, I won't need to take them for walks." She peered at her beetles through her fingers. "You doing okay, Cleitus and Cephalus?"

Artemis raised an eyebrow. "Cleitus and Cephalus?"

"Yeah, I don't really know if they're boys, but I've decided I'm naming them after these twin brothers that Tithonus hangs out with," Eos explained. "The brothers are identical. And they kind of remind me of beetles. They're roundish, and they have black hair and always wear shiny black tunics."

Athena and Artemis laughed again.

Before the three girls knew it, they were climbing the granite steps to the Academy and pushing through its bronze front doors. Before they headed upstairs to the girls' dorm, Artemis ducked into the cafeteria and grabbed an apple and an orange. "Breakfast snack, for you to take with you tomorrow morning," she told Eos.

Since the beetles were cupped in Eos's hands, Artemis slipped the apple and orange into the pockets of Eos's chiton. Together the girls climbed the marble stairs to the fourth floor.

"You'll need something to put those beetles in," Athena said when they stopped outside her and Pandora's dorm room. "I've got a glass jar you can have." She ducked inside her room and quickly returned with the jar, as well as a piece of loosely woven cloth and a string to tie the cloth over the mouth of the jar so the beetles wouldn't escape.

Athena held the jar while Eos carefully placed her beetles inside and then tied the cloth cover over the top. "Perfect. Thanks," she told Athena. Then, glancing at Artemis, too, she said, "You guys are the best. It's been sooo much fun hanging around with you!" They all hugged and said their farewells, since Athena and Artemis would likely still be sound asleep when Eos left the next morning.

Once inside Aphrodite's dark room, Eos set the jar on a desk and lit a small lamp she found there. Then she changed into the pink nightgown Aphrodite had let her borrow and tossed her chiton on top of her bag to put back on in the morning. She shifted the heart-shaped pillows to the end of the bed, but instead of climbing into it right then, she couldn't resist going back to the desk where she'd left her beetles.

She gazed at them fondly through the glass. "Nighty-night, sweetie beetelies. I'm glad Persephone and Aphrodite took their kitten home for the night. Otherwise Adonis might have tried to *eat* you!"

Speaking of eating, what if Cleitus and Cephalus were hungry? she thought anxiously. She remembered Tithonus saying that many beetles liked fruit. Hurrying over to her bag, she pulled the apple and the orange from the pockets of her chiton. At the desk again, she held both over the jar. "Which would you prefer?" she asked her beetles. "Apple? Or orange?"

"Both!" she squeaked, pretending they were replying to her question.

"You got it, my little beetle boys!" she answered them in her normal voice.

Using her fingernails, she peeled off bits of both fruits and gently placed the pieces at the bottom of the jar. "Tomorrow I'll add a few twigs to your jar in case you'd like something to climb on," she promised them. "And I'll pick some fresh grass shoots too, in case you'd like those better than fruit."

Before she blew out the lamp, Eos borrowed a

sheet of papyrus from the top of Aphrodite's desk. Quickly she wrote a note, thanking Aphrodite for letting her spend the night in her room, and for the use of one of her nightgowns. She also told Aphrodite what a good time she'd had at MOA. She decided not to mention the tension she'd sensed when they parted. If she'd been right about that, Aphrodite was probably over her anger by now, anyway.

She left the note on the desk, then slipped into bed and pulled the comforter up to her chin. Feeling as snug as a bug in a rug, she fell fast asleep.

10

Home Again

IT WAS PAST LUNCHTIME ON SUNDAY WHEN EOS arrived at the open courtyard of her home and transformed to whirl down into her urn-room. She'd waved to Nyx when she'd seen her at dawn, thanked her again for the invitation, and quickly mentioned her fun trip to the Supernatural Market last night.

Though the flight home had been long, it had given her time to think about all that had happened yesterday. Especially the surprising things Zeus had said about her dad, and the chance he'd given her to make Tithonus immortal. She'd even worked out the words to a spell that she hoped would do the trick!

After taking a shower and changing clothes in her urn-room, she checked on her beetle boys. They were perched on the twigs she'd placed inside their jar that morning. "Hey, guys, you doing okay?" she asked them. They said nothing, of course, but she noticed they'd eaten the pieces of apple and orange she'd given them before she'd gone to bed last night.

"I bet you're hungry again," she said. "I ate the rest of the apple and orange on the way home. But, good news, I saved one hunk of the orange for you guys." Taking it from a small pouch at the top of her bag, she lowered it into their jar.

"I'm hungry too," she told her beetles as they

scampered over to the piece of orange. They were so cute! Feeling a surge of affection for them, she added, "I'm going to go get some lunch, and I'll bring you sweet little beetle-tweetles another treat when I come back, okay?" Not that she expected them to answer or anything.

Once she'd covered the jar and secured the cloth with the string Athena had given her, Eos scratched at an itchy red spot that had appeared on her upper arm that morning. Hmm. Looked like some kind of bug bite. All at once she flashed on Aphrodite giggling and saying in a singsong voice, "Good night. Sleep tight. Don't let the bedbugs bite." That goddessgirl had been mega-angry with her only moments before she'd said that. What if she'd actually been casting a magic spell to cause this bite when she'd chanted that rhyme? But no, Eos told herself, that idea was just plain silly. Besides, that didn't sound like a spell to her.

In seconds Eos had transformed herself into a pink vapor again and spiraled up and out of her urn-room. Then she became her goddessgirl self and went into the kitchen.

"Oh, good. You're home! How was the sleepover?" Dressed in a glittery red chiton, her mom stood at the counter, chopping lettuce. As her knife moved up and down, the diamond bracelet on her wrist jiggled and flashed.

"Fun," Eos replied, figuring Theia didn't have time for details. As busy as she always was, she'd probably be off somewhere as soon as she'd eaten.

"I'm making a big salad for lunch. Want some?" her mom asked.

Eos nodded. "Yes, thanks." Then she added, "I

didn't expect you to be home. I thought you'd be at a meeting or out helping with one of your charities." Spying a bowl of grapes on the counter, she tossed a couple into her mouth and then stuck one in the pocket of her chiton to give to Cleitus and Cephalus later.

"I skipped my jewelry-club meeting," her mom informed her. After putting the chopped lettuce onto two plates, she began to slice up a cucumber.

Startled, Eos's mouth dropped open as she reached for more grapes. "You did? But aren't you in charge of the meetings? You're the president." She had never known her mom to blow off a commitment! The two of them were alike that way. They kept their promises, and when they said they were going to do something, they followed through.

Her mom gave her an affectionate smile. "I am. But I decided someone else could take over today's meeting. I wanted to be here to chat when you got home." She set down her knife. "In fact, I'm thinking I may cut back on some of my activities, so I can be home more often."

"Really?" Eos said, her eyebrows going up.

"Really. You're growing up so fast, and . . . well . . . I'd like to spend more time with you." Theia's forehead furrowed as she looked at Eos. "Would you like that too?"

Eos grinned. "Yeah, definitely." But then she added, "Only I wouldn't want you to give up anything you really wanted to do. I'm *proud* of the all the things you do!"

"Why, thank you, sweetie. That's good to know." Theia opened her arms to Eos, and they hugged. "I'll still keep doing the activities I enjoy most," her mom assured her afterward, while adding olives and cherry tomatoes to the salads. "It won't hurt to give up being in charge of a few, though. That'll offer others a chance to step forward and lead."

Hmm, thought Eos. *Interesting point.* If her mom could give up being in charge of some of her activities, maybe *she* could too. She might start by letting someone else take over the Scrollbook Club meetings. Her lips curled into a mischievous smile. Maybe Zoe? Then it would be that girl's turn to be annoyed when others hadn't read the month's book!

"Now tell me everything about Ephesus and your visit to Mount Olympus Academy," her mom said as they carried their salads to the table and sat down. So as they ate, Eos described Artemis's amazing temple and the unveiling of Nyx's statuette. And she told about the party, too, and how Apollo's band had played and she'd gotten to dance with other goddessgirls and godboys. "And I also met Athena's little sister, Hebe. Hera brought her." Here Eos paused and cocked her head at Theia. "How do you and Hera know each other, anyway?"

Her mom smiled. "I bought a dress from her shop in the Immortal Marketplace once, to wear to a friend's wedding." The IM was enormous, with shops that sold everything from the newest Greek fashions to tridents and thunderbolts. Hera's wedding shop was called (appropriately enough) Hera's Happy Endings. "And we also worked on a committee together a few years ago, before she and Zeus were married," Theia added.

Her mention of Zeus caused Eos to blurt out, "I saw him at MOA. He said he and Dad play chess together?"

Her mom nodded. "Mm-hm. I've visited the

Underworld a couple of times while they were playing. I would've mentioned it before, but I didn't want to break my promise to you by discussing your d—"

"But aren't you mad at Zeus?" Eos interrupted, feeling confused. "I mean, *he's* the whole reason Dad is in the Underworld. Aren't we *enemies*?"

"Enemies?" Her mom shook her head. "No, the Titanomachy was a long time ago. From the start, both sides in that war knew what the punishment would be if they lost. I don't believe in holding on to anger about the past." Having finished her salad, she set down her fork and then grinned. "Besides, your dad always beats Zeus at chess. He jokes that if a game of chess had decided who would rule, instead of that war, then he and the Titans would be in power instead of Zeus and the Olympians. Zeus may be King of the Gods, but your dad is King of the Chessboard!"

Eos laughed. She loved the idea that her dad could beat the King of the Gods at something. When she'd talked to Zeus yesterday, however, he'd been pretty confident that he'd finally win a match. But had he won?

"Zeus was nicer than I imagined he'd be," she admitted. She didn't mention that she'd asked him to make Tithonus immortal and that he'd granted her the power to do so, though. She was a little worried that her mom might not think it was a good idea. It was! But grown-ups were sometimes too cautious, in her humble opinion.

All at once Eos became aware that her mom was studying her. "What?" she said.

"I know I promised I'd never speak about your

dad to you again," her mom replied hesitantly, "but you brought him up yourself just now. And I wonder . . . would you like to go with me to the Underworld next time I visit him?"

Eos sucked in her breath. Would she? She thought about what her mom had just said about not holding on to anger. Was that what she had been doing all these years? Holding on to anger toward her dad? And toward Zeus, too? "When are you going?" she asked carefully.

"Tomorrow," Theia answered. "We could go after you're home from school. About an hour south of here by chariot there's a shortcut to Tartarus. It's within a circle of big boulders that you can see from the air. We could visit your dad and get back with plenty of time for you to do homework, if you have any."

Eos nodded and set down her napkin, finished

with eating. "I'll think about it." After all these years, she wasn't even sure what she'd say to her dad. In spite of what her mom had said, she was still kind of mad at him for not coming home after the war. He'd *promised*.

But now it occurred to her to wonder if she was being unfair. Maybe some promises just couldn't be kept. It was something to consider, anyway. She got up from the table and took her and her mom's empty salad plates over to the sink.

"Oh. I almost forgot," said Theia. "Tithonus came looking for you this morning. I told him you'd spent the night at MOA and would be home later."

"Thanks," said Eos. "I'd better go see him. I promised to help him with his science-fair project on grasshoppers." She also planned to make him immortal before her immortality-granting power could expire, but she didn't tell her mom that!

Soon Eos was off next door, taking with her the papyrus Ares had autographed, and Cleitus and Cephalus in their jar so Tithonus could meet them. When she knocked at the red door of his house, he answered almost immediately and ushered her into the living room. Posters in progress, some with diagrams and illustrations of grasshoppers, blanketed the floor. Eos edged around them, careful not to step on any.

"Wow, you've done a lot!" she told him.

Tithonus grinned at all his posters, looking pleased. "Mom hates messes. She'd have a fit if she saw I'd spread these all out here. Luckily, she went to an exercise class and has plans to attend some kind of lecture afterward. She won't be home tonight till around seven." Noticing the jar Eos was holding, a curious look came over his face. "What have you got there?" he asked.

Her eyes sparkled. "Beetles!" She removed the cloth top and held out the jar to him.

"Cool!" he said, after peering inside. "Those belong to the Tenebrionidae family of beetles."

"Ten-knee-bree-a-what?" asked Eos.

Tithonus laughed. "A more common name is *darkling* beetle."

"I like that better. Much easier to say and remember. Guess what I named them."

"Zeus and Hera?"

"Nope."

"Beetledum and Beetledee?"

She giggled. "Nope. Cleitus and Cephalus."

As she knew he would, Tithonus cracked up, getting right away why she'd named them after the twins. "I totally see the resemblance." He handed the jar back. "Are you going to keep them as pets?" he asked, reaching to straighten his untamable cowlick.

Eos nodded, gazing into the jar at her cute little fellows. "Got any beetle-care tips? I gave them some fruit, but I wasn't really sure what to feed them."

"Fruit's fine. Darkling beetles will eat a lot of different things," Tithonus told her. After selecting a few of the half-finished posters spread over the floor, he carried them to the dining room table, then pulled out a chair and sat.

Eos followed him, set her beetle jar on the table, and sat down too. She watched him pick up a pen and start adding details to a rough sketch showing the enlarged body of a grasshopper—one that looked a lot like his Melody. Since she was nowhere to be seen, Eos figured Tithonus had left her in his room for now.

"You could also feed your beetles plants, buds, grains, even dead leaves," he said as he sketched. "And you won't need to give them water. They can get all the moisture they need from the food they eat."

"Thanks," said Eos. He passed her one of the posters, and she got to work helping him with all the written parts of his project, including titles, labels, and captions. As they worked, she briefly told him about her experiences at Ephesus and MOA, and the goddessgirls and godboys she'd met. He was wildly excited when she gave him Ares' autograph. "Awesome! Cleitus and Cephalus will turn as green as . . . as *figeater* beetles when they see it!"

Eos wanted to tell him about the mighty godboy of war being afraid of spiders. Only she'd promised

Ares she wouldn't say a word about his phobia to anyone. "Sorry I didn't get you Zeus's autograph too," she said instead. So much had happened while she was in the principal's office that she'd completely forgotten to ask for it.

"S'okay," said Tithonus, all smiles. He traced a finger over Ares' signature in awe. "I'm happy just to have this one!" As the two of them went on working, Eos recited to herself over and over the immortality spell she'd composed in her head on her flight home. Tithonus was going to be sooo pleased and surprised!

When he took a break to fetch them some snacks, she made up her mind to perform the spell the moment he came back. He would surely thank her afterward. His excitement over Ares' autograph would be nothing compared to his excitement over becoming immortal. She couldn't wait!

So as soon as Tithonus reentered the dining room, holding a couple of pears, Eos stood to face him. Then she uttered these words:

> *"A mortal you'll no longer be,*
>
> *In just two minutes' time.*
>
> *I give you immortality*
>
> *Through this spell made of rhyme."*

As she'd expected, a look of surprise crossed Tithonus's face. "What did you just do?"

She grinned big. "I made you immortal. In about two minutes you'll be a godboy. Which means, like me, you'll never die. Isn't that pink?" She waited for him to get excited and thank her. Instead he frowned.

"*What?* But I don't want to be a godboy!" he

insisted. "I'm happy being a mortal and doing what I want. Short life or long life, it's the quality of life that matters."

This was hardly the reaction Eos had anticipated. "I thought everyone wished to be immortal!" she said.

"Why would you think that?" Tithonus scoffed.

Her eyes widened in astonishment. "But—but—but—" she sputtered. "Once you become a godboy we can be friends forever! Because of my spell, don't you see?"

Tithonus shook his head urgently, frowning. "Immortals have big responsibilities, and everyone is always asking them for stuff. Us mortals can choose to do whatever we care about. If you're really my friend, you'll stop this spell. Now."

Before Eos could react, the pears Tithonus was

holding dropped to the floor. *Thunk! Thunk!* She watched them roll across it as if in slow motion. When she glanced back up, it was just in time to see him shrink smaller . . . and smaller . . . until he was the size of a tiny twig. No, not a twig—a *grasshopper*! Oh no! With no time to wonder what had gone wrong, she chased after him as he hopped away. *Boing!*

"Tithonus, come back!" she yelled as he bounced around the room. "I love you!"

Huh? *"I love you"*? she mouthed silently. Why had she said that? Tithonus had told her grasshoppers could hear.

Her face turned red. "Just in case you heard that, I didn't mean it," she called toward him. "I mean, I like you, but I'm not crushing on you or anything like that."

Dimly, she recalled Athena saying that it seemed

like Eos was starting to love bugs. This was after she'd captured Cleitus and Cephalus, of course. But there was no time to ponder that now. She had to keep grasshopper-Tithonus from getting away!

He was boinging here and there, hopping from the floor to the couch to a small table, then back down to the floor and into the kitchen. Eos gave chase. Every time he landed on something new, she crept up on him and then reached out with her hands to catch him. But he was too fast for her. Each time, her hands closed on air as he escaped.

Eventually he hopped up onto a window frame. To her horror she saw that the window was open. "No! Stop! Don't leave me. Be my bug boyfriend!" *Aaagh!* What was wrong with her? She did not want a boyfriend right now! Why in the world was she saying stuff like that? But before she could shoo

Tithonus away from the window and close it, he hopped outside.

Eos's heart plummeted. She couldn't lose him! He might not be her bug boyfriend, but he *was* her best friend!

"Stay right there!" she shouted, hoping against hope that he might understand her and do as she asked. Racing out the door, she ran around to the outside of the house. She breathed a sigh of relief when she saw grasshopper-Tithonus clinging to a bush just below the open window. She crept closer, hands reaching.

Suddenly, Bugs appeared. *Meow!* Eyeing the grasshopper, Tithonus's cat crouched to pounce on it.

"Nooo!" wailed Eos. She flung herself at the surprised fur ball. *Meow! Hiss!* Startled, the cat shot under the house.

Boing! Grasshopper-Tithonus hopped away again. Eos's eyes stayed glued to him as she trailed him across the backyard. "Come back!" she begged. "Remember how you told me grasshoppers usually only live for a couple of months in the wild? Remember spiders, birds, snakes, and rodents? Plus *cats*? They think grasshoppers are dinner! Trust me, you will not be hoppy, er, happy out here. This backyard spells bad news for you, pal."

Oh, why hadn't her spell worked the way she'd intended? What had she done wrong? And how could she make it right? If only she could reverse the spell and make Tithonus himself again!

Eventually, grasshopper-Tithonus came to rest

on a stalk of grass at the edge of the field behind the house. Eos drew in her breath. This could be her last chance to catch him. If he bounded into that tall grass, it would be bye-bye Bug Boy forever!

Her heart beat fast and her hands shook as she brought them down around the grasshopper. Slowly . . . slowly . . .

"Gotcha!" she crowed happily.

But as she opened her hands a crack to peek at him, Tithonus boinged up between her fingers and hopped away. With a howl of dismay, she plowed through the tall grass after him, calling out to him over and over.

"Tithonus! Where are you? Please come back!" As she frantically crashed through the field, dozens more grasshoppers sprang up around her.

She felt her heart break. He could be any or none of them.

Eos sank down onto the grass. Wrapping her arms around her knees, she dropped her head forward and sobbed.

11

Crossed Spells

SEVERAL MINUTES PASSED BEFORE EOS REALIZED that something was tickling her cheek. Slowly she raised her head. The tickling stopped. She looked around her. Then, suddenly, a grasshopper hopped onto one of her knees.

She stared at it. "Tithonus? Is that you?" The grasshopper stared back at her. It *looked* like the same grasshopper she'd been chasing. And it was clearly male, since it was smaller than she remembered Melody being. Hope rose inside her. She grew even more certain it was the right grasshopper when affection for the little guy surged through her.

"I think it is you. 'Cause you're cute as a bug's ear!" (Another of Tithonus's bug sayings.) Eos's heart pounded with joy. But, just to be sure, she said, "If it *is* you, Tithonus, give me a sign. Wave one of your little antennae or something." At first the grasshopper remained still, continuing to stare at her. But then, very slowly, it lifted a hind leg and rubbed it against a wing. *Chirp!*

She was so happy she could've *hugged* the grasshopper. Only she'd be afraid of crushing him. "I'm so sorry about that spell," she told him, in case he really could understand her. "I'll find a way to fix things. I promise!" Until she did, her heart would never feel light again!

With her palm turned up, she reached out to him. "Hop on. Please," she begged. "I need to stash you in a safe place until I can figure out what went wrong with the spell I cast to try to make you immortal."

Her mind raced. Maybe Zeus had never really had any intention of allowing her to make Tithonus immortal. Had he only agreed as some cruel trick, knowing her spell wouldn't work? But she dismissed these thoughts as quickly as they had come. Zeus had seemed to hold no hard feelings toward her family. He even played chess with her dad! And hadn't Zeus warned her that immortality spells were tricky? No, the fault must lie with her spell somehow.

As she was pondering this, the grasshopper hopped from her knee to the palm of her hand. She gently cupped her other hand over the top of him and then rose to her feet.

Back at Tithonus's house, she went straight to his room. A small terrarium sat on his desk. There was dirt in the bottom of it, but Tithonus hadn't added any plants—or Melody—yet. For now, Melody's covered jar sat on some bookshelves at the foot of his bed.

Speaking through the fingers of her cupped hands to grasshopper-Tithonus, Eos asked, "Want to share Melody's jar for just a little while? Maybe you could chirp-ask her to share some bug—er, insect—secrets."

Chirp!

"I'll take that as a 'yes,'" Eos replied. But then an unexpected pang of jealousy pierced her heart. What if while chirping along together Tithonus and

Melody became BFFs, or Melody started crushing on Tithonus? She mentally rolled her eyes at herself for worrying about this. Was she going totally buggy, or what?

Maybe she could put him in the jar with Cleitus and Cephalus instead, she thought. But she wasn't sure if that would be a good idea either. Did beetles and grasshoppers get along? "Changed my mind," she told grasshopper-Tithonus. "I think you need your own place." So saying, she held her hands over the unfinished terrarium and released him into it. Then she grabbed a good-size dictionary from one of the bookshelves and used it to cover the top of the terrarium. That would keep him from escaping until she could find a way to remove her spell.

She carried the terrarium back into the living room and set it on the dining room table. Then she took a sheet of papyrus and scribbled a note to Tithonus's mother, saying that she and he were going to her house and would have dinner over there. She didn't add that Tithonus was now a grasshopper. Definitely TMI.

It had taken weeks to regain Tithonus's mom's trust so that she would allow Eos and Tithonus to play together again after what had happened with Nefili in second grade. If his mom found out about this, it would likely take *years* till they were allowed to hang out again. She only had this evening to fix her spell-gone-wrong.

Leaving the note in an easy-to-notice place on the table, Eos then tidied up. She gathered all the posters, pens, and supplies together and placed them beside her note. She picked up the two pears that had fallen to the floor when Tithonus had transformed into a grasshopper and took them back to the kitchen.

"Okay, let's go," she said at last to her three bug boyfriends. Balancing the jar with the beetles on top of the dictionary-covered terrarium with grasshopper-Tithonus, she carefully carried everything outside and over to her house.

Somehow she managed to make it through her front door and into the courtyard without running into her mom. There she set her stuff down for just a minute so she could pick a few blades of grass from the garden. These she dropped into the terrarium after sliding the dictionary to one side.

She was standing before her decorated terra-cotta urn, about to twirl in circles to vaporize and zoom herself, the jar, and the terrarium into her room, when something whooshed from the sky into the courtyard. *Thump!* A winged notescroll dropped to land at her feet. *Huh?*

Wondering who it could be from, she briefly set down her bug-load to pick it up. But instead of unrolling it to read then and there, she tucked it under her arm, since she heard her mom coming. After picking up the terrarium and jar again, she twirled herself and them into a pink vapor. *Whoosh!* Down they all went through the top of the urn.

Once she became her goddess self again, Eos set everything on the desk in her urn-room. A quick rummage through her pink-painted ward-robe yielded an old knitted scarf she rarely wore. After sliding the dictionary onto her desk, she draped the scarf over the open terrarium and then taped the scarf's edges to the glass to make it stay in place. Perfect! This woven lid would keep grasshopper-Tithonus inside while also letting in some air.

That done, Eos grabbed the notescroll, untied the sparkly pink ribbon from around it, and sank down on the edge of her bed to read it. As if the border of pink and red hearts around the note weren't enough of a clue to the sender's identity, Aphrodite had also signed her name in a large, loopy script at the bottom of the scroll, dotting the *i* with a little heart. Eos flicked a glance at the terrarium, and then began reading.

> *Dear Eos,*
>
> *I am just back from Persephone's. I wanted to let you know that Ares told me the truth about his fear of spiders and how he asked you to identify an enormous, poisonous-looking spider in his room.*

"Enormous"? "Poisonous-looking"? A giggle escaped Eos. Apparently Ares hadn't been *entirely* truthful with Aphrodite. But good for him for admitting his spider phobia! She went on reading:

He said the two of you got rid of it, so thank you!

The TWO of them got rid of it? She giggled again.

I owe you a huge apology. I'm embarrassed
to admit that I thought you and Ares were
crushing, so I let my jealous temperament get the
better of me and summoned a bedbug to bite you.
I hope the itching has finally gone away!

Eos looked up from the note in surprise. So her "silly" idea about Aphrodite being responsible for the bug bite had been right after all. Aphrodite's rhyming chant had brought forth the bug! Luckily, the bite had stopped itching. She glanced at her arm and saw that the red spot was hardly noticeable now. "No real harm done," she murmured. She went back to reading the notescroll:

> *And I'm also sorry to say that before you went off*
>
> *to the Supernatural Market, I cast a spell on you.*

"Huh?" Eos's eyes widened in alarm as she read on, learning the exact words of that spell:

> *From among the bugs you see,*
>
> *You will fall in love with three.*
>
> *While this spell is in effect,*

Other spells will redirect.

These love bugs you must protect!

Some spell, thought Eos. More like a curse! And what did it mean, exactly? Aphrodite's note didn't explain, but it did finish up with some helpful info:

After you start to crush on a third and final bug, this spell will be complete and your love for bugs will ease. That easing may take several hours, though. I am truly sorry for what I did. I hope you can forgive me.

Sincerely,

Aphrodite

P.S. Thanks for the thank-you note you left on my desk. I really hope we'll meet again someday.

215

By the end of the notescroll, Eos's thoughts were whirling. Her sudden crush on this bug-boyfriend trio finally made sense. She was so relieved about that that she was already feeling forgiveness toward Aphrodite. At least that goddessgirl had owned up to what she'd done and that it was wrong. Still, the second-to-last line of Aphrodite's spell remained puzzling. What did it mean that while the love-bug spell was in effect, other spells would "redirect"?

She began to put her thoughts in order. It was clear that Aphrodite's spiteful spell had been "in effect" when Eos cast her immortality spell on Tithonus. So her immortality spell must have been "redirected." But what exactly did that mean?

"I need a dictionary!" she said out loud.

She slid off her bed and went over to her desk.

Wiggling his antennae, grasshopper-Tithonus watched her through the glass of his terrarium as she thumbed through the dictionary she'd taken from Tithonus's room till she came to the *R*s.

"Here it is," she murmured. "'Redirect' means to direct something to a new place or purpose. So what if my spell was 'redirected' to the new purpose of turning you into my third love bug? Oh no! If Aphrodite's spell and mine got tangled together, maybe I made you not just a grasshopper, but an *immortal* grasshopper! Doomed to bugdom forever!"

Her forehead furrowed as she stared at grasshopper-Tithonus. Crazy as it seemed, that might just be the case! But as to why Tithonus had become a grasshopper instead of some other kind of bug, she had no idea. Maybe the spell had just chosen the bug it sensed Tithonus liked best.

The problem now was how to *redirect* the redirect, to change Tithonus back into himself again. She couldn't just assume that as Aphrodite's spell "eased" off her, it would also change him back to a boy. In fact, that didn't seem likely, since her spell had said nothing about changing a boy to a bug to begin with. With a sinking feeling, she realized she had neither the knowledge nor the skill to fix things. She was pretty sure her mom didn't either.

Abruptly, she remembered her dad's spell-casting award out in the courtyard. Hmm. Should she? Left no other choice, she made up her mind at once.

"I'm going to go visit my dad in the Underworld," she told grasshopper-Tithonus, who was busy nibbling on one of the blades of grass she'd pulled up for him. "He might be able to teach me a spell to fix things."

Grasshopper-Tithonus paused his chewing to study her intently. "I wish I could take you with me, but I can't risk it," Eos told him. Then she cooed, "Because the Underworld is not a safe place for the besty-westy widdle love bug ever!"

Her grasshopper friend cocked his head at her as if to say, *You are acting weird, girl!* And she knew she was. *Aargh!* Embarrassed at what she'd just said, Eos told him, "Don't worry. When Aphrodite's spell finally wears off, I should go back to being my normal self, I hope." Meaning she'd no longer adore three bug boys.

"Mom?" she called, as soon as she was out of her urn. No reply. Eos raced around the house calling for her until she spotted a note on the kitchen counter:

Gone grocery shopping. Need to stop to see a sick friend on my way back. So sorry, but dinner will be late. ~ Mom

While it was nice of her mother—and very like her—to take time to visit a sick friend, Eos couldn't help wishing Theia were coming straight home after shopping. Because she couldn't wait around to ask her mom if it was okay for her to fly to the Underworld.

A peek at the garden sundial showed that it was almost five in the afternoon. Only a couple of hours till Tithonus's mother would get back. *Ye gods!* Eos knew from past experience that his mom would expect him home no later than nine, since it was a school night. She would not be happy if she had to come looking for him, only to discover he was a grasshopper! If that happened, even if Eos did eventually manage to change him back to a boy, it might not just take years before Tithonus's mom would let them be friends again. She might forbid Eos to ever see him again!

For Eos to get to the Underworld and back before nightfall, with time to perform the spell she hoped to get from her dad, she needed to leave *now*. Quickly she scribbled a note to her mom, explaining that—surprise, surprise—she'd gone off to see her dad today, instead of waiting until tomorrow. She grabbed some snacks and her cloak and was off.

Her wings were still tired from her earlier trip home from Mount Olympus Academy, leaving her little energy for vaporizing. Fortunately, she remembered the shortcut to Tartarus her mom had told her about, and she could fly almost as quickly as a chariot could soar. Although the shortcut was well-hidden at ground level, she was easily able to spot it from the air after flying for about an hour. Within a circle of huge, jagged boulders she saw the wide crack in the earth. Diving through the crack, Eos whooshed down, down, down, entering a dark abyss.

12

Tartarus

IT SEEMED LIKE FOREVER BEFORE EOS LANDED
at the bottom of the pit that was Tartarus, the deep-
est place in the Underworld. A murky gloom hung
over the pit. She shivered in the dank air as she
folded back her wings and then wrapped her cloak
tightly around her. Having no map to guide her, she
chose a path along the side of the pit and began to
walk over the damp and stony ground.

A few minutes into her walk she spied a gaunt shade (as human souls in the Underworld were called) rolling a large boulder ahead of him. When he reached a certain spot, he braced his back against the boulder and tried, grunting and groaning, to push it up the side of the pit. But despite his effort, he could only force the heavy-looking boulder a mere foot or so up the steep wall before the rock rolled back down again. He ran after it and began to push it again.

"You're not trying to push that rock out of the pit, are you?" Eos called out to the shade as she drew closer to him.

With a resigned air, he paused in his pushing to nod at her.

"That'll never work," she told him firmly. "But if you could build some kind of pulley system, you might be able to hoist it up with that."

The shade shook his head. "Helpful machinery not allowed. Forever failing to get that wretched rock out of this wretched pit is my punishment."

"Oh!" Eos said. Since Tartarus was where the truly evil wound up, not just those who were prisoners of war like her dad, she guessed she should have realized this was a punishment. As she was wondering what horrible deeds had landed this particular shade here, he gave her a smile that was more like a grimace and added, "Name's Sisyphus,"

"I'm Eos," she replied. "Goddessgirl of the dawn."

He nodded. "I could tell you weren't a shade. Not with those wings of yours." Even though she'd folded them back, they still stuck out a little under her cloak.

"I'm looking for my father," she explained. "Do you know him? His name's Hyperion."

"Not much socializing here in Tartarus," Sisyphus remarked. "No parties being thrown, that's for sure." For a moment his brow furrowed. "I've heard of him, though. He's one of the Titans, right?"

Eos nodded eagerly. "Yes. Where can I find him?"

Sisyphus shrugged. "No clue. Good luck, though." And with that he went back to pushing his boulder.

Well, that was disappointing. Pink vapor trailed from Eos's fingertips as she lifted her hand to wave good-bye. She continued over the stony ground, through patches of thick mist that often obscured her path so that she had to pick her way slowly and carefully to avoid stumbling. This place was more than a little scary.

When she came upon a post with multiple location signs pointing in various directions, she stood and read some of the gloomy-sounding names: the

Tower of Torment, the Mound of Misery, the Area of Anguish, and so forth. Where might her father be? Maybe in the Home of Hotheads? The Domicile of Dads? The Residence of Rebels? If only she knew where exactly Nyx lived here in Tartarus. Maybe she'd know where to find him. Unfortunately, though, they had never thought to exchange addresses.

Suddenly, from out of the mist, a bearded man with a clipboard appeared. He frowned at her. "Excuse me, but who are you and what are you doing here?" he asked in a brisk voice. The name tag pinned to his tunic identified him as Hypnos.

Eos's face broke into a relieved smile. "I know who you are!"

The man rolled his eyes. "Was the name tag a clue?"

Even though she was pretty sure Hypnos hadn't

meant to be funny, she let out a giggle. "I'm Eos. Goddessgirl of the Dawn. A friend of Nyx's."

Like the sun breaking through storm clouds, Hypnos was suddenly all smiles and warmth. "Sure! Nyx told me and my brother all about you. Any friend of hers is a friend of ours. So are you here to visit Nyx?" he asked, shifting his clipboard under one arm.

It suddenly occurred to Eos that if she started visiting her dad down here in future, she could also visit Nyx. Pink! "Not this time," she replied. "I came to see my dad . . . only I'm not sure where to find him."

Hypnos's eyebrows rose. "And his name is . . . ?"

"Hyperion," Eos told him.

Hypnos's eyebrows rose even higher. But all he said was, "Follow me," before immediately striking out in the direction of the sign pointing toward the Ditch of Despair.

Eos shivered. Was that where her dad was?

"We don't get many visitors here in the Underworld," Hypnos told Eos as she struggled to keep up with his fast pace. "Especially not in Tartarus. I've seen your mom here often enough, though. And Zeus has been coming to see your dad a lot lately too. Cocky when he arrives, but pouting when he leaves. Your dad is one wicked chess champ!"

Pride swelled in Eos that all of Underworld thought well of her dad—or at least of his chess-playing skill. Turned out that the Ditch of Despair, filled with murky water and smelling of rotting fish, wasn't their final destination. Holding her nose as she went past it, Eos followed Hypnos to a surprisingly cozy-looking little whitewashed cottage nestled between two large boulders. Star-shaped white flowers grew in pots on either side of the cottage's cheery yellow front door.

"Give my regards to your dad," Hypnos said, going no farther. "A boatload of shades being ferried up the River Styx is due to arrive soon, and I've got to go sort them out. Have a good visit!" He dipped his head in farewell, turned on his heel, and scurried away.

Standing there before the door, Eos grew anxious. She wished Hypnos hadn't gone off and left her to face her father alone. What if her dad didn't recognize her? He hadn't seen her since she was a toddler, after all. If it weren't for the painted portrait of him that her mom kept on her bedside table at home, Eos wouldn't know him, either.

Gathering all her courage, she straightened, and then knocked at the door.

"Coming!" a deep voice called out.

Soon the door opened to reveal a tall, lean man wearing a midnight blue robe patterned with white stars. Though his hair had some gray in it now compared to the picture on her mom's bedside table, Eos recognized him instantly.

"Yes?" He squinted at her and then asked in a polite voice, "May I help you?"

Her heart fell. He didn't know her. "Dad?" she said.

A startled look flashed in his eyes. Then a broad smile spread over his face. "Eos? Is it really you? Sorry, I don't have my glasses on."

So it was just that, not that he'd forgotten her. What a relief! She nodded, suddenly feeling shy. "Yes, it's me," she replied.

"Come in, come in," he said, holding the door wide open. "It's so great to see my youngest daughter after all these long years!"

Eos tensed. Was he trying to make her feel guilty about not coming to see him till now? She felt a spark of anger. Two could play at that game. How about all those missed birthdays and other special occasions? No card from him? No letterscroll? But she saw only joy in his eyes, and her annoyance vanished.

As she entered the cottage, she looked around. The furnishings inside were sparse: a small couch and coffee table, a couple of straight-backed chairs, and a desk with a shelf above it that held a few books. She supposed there must be a tiny bedroom and bath beyond the door at one side of the cottage. Only two items in the main room really stood out—the chess set occupying the coffee table and a telescope that sat before the cottage's back window.

"I have something urgent to ask," Eos said, getting right to the point. "I've made kind of a terrible mistake, and I need help."

Her dad's forehead creased with concern. He gestured toward the couch before reaching for a pair of glasses on the coffee table. "Please," he said as he slipped on the glasses. "Have a seat. Then you can tell me what the trouble is."

"Thanks, but I . . . um . . . can't stay long," she murmured, shifting from one foot to the other.

Instantly, disappointment clouded her dad's face. "Oh." But then he smiled again. "How can I help?"

Relenting a little, she perched on the edge of the couch. Her dad pulled one of the straight-backed chairs near and sat too. "I've made a big mess of things," she confessed in a rush. And then, without warning, tears sprang from her eyes.

"There, there," her dad said kindly. "Things can't be all that bad, can they?" Reaching out, he clumsily patted her arm.

Eos wiped away her tears with the back of her hand. "I came here thinking you might be able to help me. I mean, because you won that spell-casting trophy in our courtyard," she began. Then, in fits and starts, she told him all about Tithonus and her botched spell and how she was hoping he could give her a spell to make Tithonus a boy again. Her dad listened attentively.

Her chin lifted toward the chess set nearby. "I hear you're a master at chess," she added brightly, just in case flattery would make him more likely to help. She didn't really know him well enough to judge. "Zeus told me that himself, when I saw him at MOA yesterday." She was aware that she was rambling, but she wanted her dad to understand that, although she'd come to him because she needed his help, she really was interested in becoming reacquainted with him.

"Not sure if I'd call myself a *master* at chess," Hyperion said humbly. Eyes twinkling, he added, "But I *am* good enough to beat Zeus, despite his recent tournament practice!" He bent his tall frame toward her. "And it's true that I have some talent for spell-casting. So, yes, I can give you a spell to turn your friend into a boy again."

"You can?" Hope bloomed in Eos's chest.

"Yes," her dad repeated. "But understand that my spell will totally reverse things. He'll become both a boy *and a mortal* again," he warned. "Casting or even just maintaining an immortality spell is not within my power."

Eos swallowed hard. "I understand." Although it seemed she'd blown her one chance to make Tithonus immortal, she would rather he was a mortal boy than an immortal grasshopper!

"Tithonus told me he thought that the quality of life was more important than the number of years lived," she confessed.

As soon as she said this, she wished she could *un*say it. Her dad had lived a lot of years, but he'd been imprisoned for much of that time. So could anyone call the quality of his life good? Yes, compared to Sisyphus, he'd gotten off easy, punishment-wise, but still . . .

"Your friend sounds very wise," her dad said, interrupting her thoughts. He rose and went to his desk. From a drawer he took out a piece of papy-rus and a feather pen. "It would help to know both your spell and Aphrodite's, since we want to uncross them," he told her.

After she recited both for him, he wrote down a *new* spell and handed it to her. "This should do the trick."

"Thank you sooo much." Eos clasped the papyrus to her chest, relieved and grateful. Anxious to get home and make Tithonus a boy again before it got super late and his mom came looking for him (and also before the easing off of Aphrodite's spell could cause any *new* problems), she folded the sheet and slipped it into the pocket of her chiton.

She rose from the couch and said, "Guess I'd bet-ter go now."

Hyperion got to the door first and held it open

for her. "Thanks for coming," he said as she came up to him. There was a hopeful note in his voice as he asked, "Will I see you again soon?"

Eos thought about what her mom had said about not holding on to anger about the past. Was she finally ready to let go of her anger at her dad for breaking his promise to come home after the war? She'd discovered for herself, that despite a person's best intentions, some promises would always get broken. She'd come very close to harming Tithonus, for example. Even though she'd promised herself after the Nefili incident at school that she'd never harm another mortal again.

She looked at her dad. He was smiling at her with hope in his twinkling eyes. He'd been willing to help her today, no questions asked. And she liked him. He was her dad. So maybe she was ready to forgive him. That maybe quickly turned into a probably, which then flipped to a yes.

Yes, she was ready to forgive and really did want to get to know him.

"Mom's coming here tomorrow. I'll go with her after school lets out," she told him.

Her dad's face brightened. "Excellent! I'll want to hear how things went with your bug-boyfriend when I see you. And maybe we can play chess."

"I don't know how."

He laughed. "No problem. I'll teach you!"

Eos smiled shyly as she took a step toward the door. Then, on an impulse, she turned back. "I wish you didn't have to live in Tartarus. I've been mad at you for not coming home like you promised."

A look of pain flashed over her dad's face. "Unfortunately, it was a promise I couldn't keep.

I'm very sorry for that, but rules are rules." After a moment's pause, he added, "It's not so bad being here, though I'd rather be at home with you and your mom, of course. I miss you both, and Helios and Selene, too." Then, as if guessing what had prompted her outburst, he added, "But even here in Tartarus I can live a life of quality. I keep busy, always learning. And I take pleasure in sharing that knowledge."

He pointed toward his telescope. "Being here has given me plenty of time to observe the movements of Helios's sun and Selene's moon, for example. I'm able to view the sky through a crack above Tartarus, and I've charted the movements of many heavenly bodies and shared my findings with others. I've also mapped the constellations. My favorite is Orion. With those three super-bright stars that make up its belt, it's as much of a show-off as that famous teen actor it's named after!"

Eos laughed. It seemed that she and her dad had similar feelings about the real Orion. And it struck her that her dad's enthusiasm for studying the heavens was just like Tithonus's enthusiasm for studying bugs. Regret washed over her for all the missed years they could've been seeing each other. She could've already been learning some of the stuff he was talking about!

Throwing her arms around him, she gave him a big hug. "Gotta fly! See you tomorrow."

A soft light had come into her dad's eyes. "Tomorrow," he echoed.

Once outside the cottage door, Eos quickly unfurled her wings and flew back the way she'd come. The sun was setting when she rose upward through the crack between the Underworld and

Earth. High above, she saw Nyx flying her chariot across the sky, her cape billowing out behind her. Already it was causing the deep yellow, orange, and red of the sunset to darken to lush violet. Soon the sky would turn midnight blue and, finally, black.

Eos waved to her friend and then continued toward home. She looked forward to telling Nyx that since she planned to visit her dad in the Underworld from time to time, she could also hang out with Nyx while there. Then they could become better friends. *Pink!*

Her mom wasn't yet home, so Eos crumpled the note she'd written her and tossed it in the trash. Out in the courtyard, she whirled into her urn, picked up the terrarium containing Tithonus and the jar containing Cleitus and Cephalus, and exited her urn-room with them.

Outside in the courtyard again she immediately turned Cleitus and Cephalus loose in her mom's flowerbed. "Have a good life," she told them. She never would have been able to release them if she'd still been bug-crushing, she realized. So Aphrodite's spell on her was definitely easing. *Phew!*

Bugs would never be her passion, she decided as she watched the beetles scurry under a rosebush. Not the way they were for Tithonus, anyway. Unlike him, she didn't yet have an intense and prolonged interest in something, which would mark it as a passion. Then again, she was only twelve. There was plenty of time to discover her true interests, right?

In the meantime she could keep trying new things. She found herself hoping, however, that a little of her increased interest in bugs, awakened by

Aphrodite's spell, would remain. Because bugs—er, insects—were pretty pink, actually!

Her thoughts were interrupted by a knock at the door. "Theia? Eos?" someone shouted. Standing in the courtyard, Eos looked over at the terrarium sitting a few feet away and froze. *Oh no!* It was Tithonus's mom outside on their front porch. And she'd be expecting to see Tithonus! As a boy, not a bug.

"Be there in a minute!" Eos called out. Hurriedly, she reached into the pocket of her chiton and drew out the spell her dad had written down. Then she uncovered the terrarium.

"Come out, Tithonus," she hissed in a low voice, so his mom wouldn't hear. Grasshopper-Tithonus didn't budge. She looked toward their front door worriedly. "Hurry up, Bug Boy. We can't let your mom see you like this." No movement. Maybe he didn't trust her. If so, who could blame him after what she'd done?

Eos waved the slip of paper where he could see it. "Get a move on! Please! My dad gave me this spell to debug you. I can't make you a boy while you're in the terrarium, though. You wouldn't fit. And your mom is about to come in our front door any minute!"

At this grasshopper-Tithonus finally bent his hind legs. *Boing!* He sprang up and over the side of the terrarium, landing a mere foot or two from her. Wasting no time, she rattled off the spell:

> *"From other spells you are set free.*
> *Including immortality.*
> *This new spell will spark reform*
> *And return you to your mortal form."*

Instantly, in a burst of what looked like green glitter, Tithonus shed his grasshopper skin. Then he grew larger and larger, until he was his normal size again, dressed in the same clothes he'd been wearing when she'd changed him into a bug. And just in time, too!

"Hi, you two. The door was unlocked, so I let myself in," his mom said as she entered the courtyard. "How's the project going?"

When Tithonus didn't speak up right away, Eos answered for the two of them. "Fine," she said, smiling weakly.

Speaking to Tithonus directly now, his mom asked, "You ready to come home? It's nearly nine, and tomorrow's a school day, you know."

"Uh, sure," he said, sounding a little dazed. "I'll hop on home in a few minutes."

Hop? Eos giggled nervously.

"Phew! That was a close call," she told him, once his mom was gone. "Are you hungry?" They never had had dinner, though she'd had some snacks at least.

"Not really," Tithonus answered. "Those blades of grass I ate as a grasshopper were surprisingly filling."

Suddenly remembering all the things she'd said to him when she was in love with bugs, she blushed. "I . . . um . . . Aphrodite's spell made me say some strange things. I mean, we're best friends and all, but not . . ." Her words stumbled to a halt when she noticed that Tithonus was blushing too.

"S'okay," he told her. "Understood."

Phew. Bracing herself to receive his wrath, she told him, "So . . . you're not just a boy again; you're also back to being mortal. My dad's spell made sure of that. I won't blame you if you're mad at me, though. Are you?"

To her surprise and delight, Tithonus beamed happily at her. "Mad? No way! That was the coolest experience ever! I don't just know *about* grasshoppers now; I know how it actually feels to *be* one! Thanks, Busy Bee."

13

The Science Fair

THERE WAS A BIG CROWD AROUND TITHONUS'S science-fair display table when Eos came by after track practice the following Friday afternoon. It was one of about fifty such tables arranged in rows throughout the Oceanus Middle School gymnasium. Five days had passed since he'd been debugged. They'd worked together every day after school that week on an exhibit that featured many hand-drawn

posters, including a grasshopper life-cycle chart, and the terrarium in which Melody now lived.

The terrarium was much nicer than when Tithonus had stayed in it. He'd added lots of edible plants and climbable twigs—things he knew from personal experience that a grasshopper like Melody would enjoy.

Eos and Tithonus had gotten to school early that morning to assemble the display. Inspired by his *transformative* experience, Eos had come up with a catchy title for their exhibit: Hoppy Days: My Life as a Grasshopper. These words were spelled out in sparkly green letters on a banner they'd hung from the ceiling over Tithonus's head. Both their names were prominently printed on it. He had insisted on adding her as cocreator of the exhibit.

"Hey, Bug Boy," she greeted him as she joined

him behind the display table and under the banner to help answer questions from students and adults who stopped by. Though Bug Boy had always been her nickname for him, now it *really* fit, since he'd actually been one.

News of Tithonus's hours-long transformation into a grasshopper had spread quickly throughout the school. Mainly because he had been so enthusiastic about the experience that he couldn't stop talking about it. For this week, anyway, it had made the two of them famous!

Since so many people at school knew about the transformation, they'd been worried that the story would eventually get back to their moms. So a few days after it happened, they'd confessed their tale. Both moms had been shocked, of course. But luckily, they'd calmed down quickly. "I know you meant well. And Tithonus did enjoy the experience," his mom had said to Eos. "But I want you to promise that you'll never cast a spell on my son ever again."

"Or on anyone else, for that matter," Eos's mom had added.

"I promise," she'd murmured. She would do her best to keep that promise too.

A boy came over to their booth now and cocked his head in question at Tithonus. "Did becoming a grasshopper change you in any permanent way? Physically, that is?"

"Sure, don't you see the antennae poking up through my hair?" Tithonus replied.

The boy looked startled, eyeing Tithonus's head.

Tithonus chuckled. "Just joking." The boy laughed. So did Eos and all the others who'd been close enough to hear. "Actually," Tithonus added after a pause, "there is one for-real change in me."

Huh? Eos swung around to look at him. "What change? You never said anything about a change!"

Waggling his eyebrows mischievously, Tithonus informed her, "Just figured it out this morning. Want to see what I can do?"

"Yes! Show us!" a girl called out. "Show us!" chimed in several more voices.

"Sure. Watch this." Tithonus came out from behind the table. "Clear the aisle!" he commanded. Immediately people moved aside to create space. Along with the others, Eos watched as, standing in the aisle now, he bent his knees.

"I can juuuuuump!" Tithonus yelled. Then, without even taking a running start, he boinged, grasshopper style. Everyone stared in astonishment as he sailed through the air to land some thirty feet farther down the aisle. For a few seconds, a stunned silence fell. Then, as he walked back, the entire gymnasium erupted in cheers. Eos just stood there, eyes wide with surprise.

A tall, athletic girl named Kareena from Eos's track team sidled up to her after this demonstration of Tithonus's extraordinary new skill. "Wait till Coach Megalos hears about this. She'll want to recruit Tithonus for the long jump!"

Eos laughed. "I bet you're right!"

"Cool!" Tithonus said, overhearing the two girls as he went to stand behind the display table again. "I always wanted to be good at some kind of sport!" He smiled at Eos. "And now, thanks to you, I am."

"Hmm," Kareena said to Eos. "I don't suppose you could cast a spell on me that would make me run faster?"

Eos shook her head, smiling. "Sorry. I had to promise both Tithonus's mom and mine that I wouldn't cast any more spells on anyone."

Another girl called to Kareena just then. Nodding at Eos before taking off, she said, "'Kay. See you at Monday's practice!"

"Yeah! Later," Eos called after her.

Eventually the science fair wound down and it was time to leave. Eos had told her mom she wouldn't be home too late, since they were planning to make dinner together tonight. Catching Tithonus's eye as he answered a student's question about Melody, she jerked her chin toward the gymnasium door. *See you*, she mouthed, and he nodded back.

She hoped that when she got home, she'd find a scroll message from her dad with a new chess move. He was teaching her to play the game, and she was already getting good at it. In addition to the one in-person game they'd played so far in the Underworld, they were also playing a "distance" game. The way this worked was she'd make a move on the at-home chessboard her mom had gotten for her. Then she'd describe the move in a message-scroll she'd send to her dad. As soon as he received the scroll, he'd make a move on his board and send a message back to her.

An unexpected side benefit of playing chess was that it seemed to calm her flighty mind and help her to focus better. To Eos's surprise, after only a few days of play she was developing a real passion for the game. Her dad was convinced that one day she would beat him. And that was something even the King of the Gods and Ruler of the Heavens couldn't do!

As she neared the gymnasium doors, she thought about the spell Kareena had requested. Probably a good thing she'd promised not to cast any more of them on anyone, she realized. Otherwise, she might be *swamped* by requests.

Being the only goddessgirl among mortals would always make her different and an outsider to some extent, Eos thought. That was just the way it was. Tithonus had told her it was a waste of time to wish for things that couldn't be. So, instead of down-playing her differentness, maybe she'd try being herself from now on. Only she would try to be smart about it and not use her powers in anger.

Everyone at this school would just have to get used to the *real* her. After all, if she could excuse Pheme for acting according to her nature as the goddessgirl of gossip and excuse Aphrodite for being jealous as was part of her nature, surely her fellow classmates could cut *her* some slack. This decision made, she smiled to herself, feeling freer and, well, more *lighthearted* than she had in quite a while!

Usually she kept her wings folded till she was out of sight of the school. But now, even before she was completely out of the gymnasium doors, she began to unfurl them. And as soon as she was outside, she let them flap. Some of the kids from her book club were standing nearby and looked up in surprise as she soared into the air. Eos just kept flying like it was no big deal. "Have a good weekend!" she yelled down to them, waving.

"You too!" they yelled, waving back.

She smiled to herself and flew onward. *Pink!*

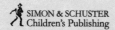

Goddess Girls

READ ABOUT ALL YOUR FAVORITE GODDESSES!

**#16 MEDUSA
THE RICH**

**#17 AMPHITRITE
THE BUBBLY**

**#18 HESTIA
THE INVISIBLE**

**#19 ECHO
THE COPYCAT**

**#20 CALLIOPE
THE MUSE**

**#21 PALLAS
THE PAL**

**#22 NYX
THE MYSTERIOUS**

**#23 MEDEA
THE ENCHANTRESS**

EBOOK EDITIONS ALSO AVAILABLE

From Aladdin
simonandschuster.com/kids